L.A. Affair

KRISS RUDOLPH

L.A. Affair

Translated by Jeffrey Essmann

BRUNO GMÜNDER

L.A. Affair
Copyright © 2011 Bruno Gmünder Verlag GmbH
Kleiststraße 23-26, 10787 Berlin, Germany
info@brunogmuender.com

Original title: L.A. Affäre
Copyright © Kriss Rudolph 2003

Translated by Jeffrey Essmann

Cover art: Henning Wossidlo
Cover photo: Copyright © David Vance
www.davidvanceprints.com

Printed in South Korea

ISBN: 978-3-86787-086-3

More information about Bruno Gmünder books and authors:
www.brunogmuender.com

for Karen

PROLOGUE

"Ben, would you please let go of that book!" Paula yelled behind me.

As I looked at her over my shoulder, she was pulling her yellow-green crocheted cap lower over her face to protect herself against the cold wind and steady drizzle, shifting from one leg to the other. She looked at me reproachfully.

"It belongs to the woman now. She just gave you a mark for it, or have you forgotten already?"

Paula didn't get it at all. It was one of my favorite books: *A History of the World in Ten and a Half Chapters* by Julian Barnes. Every single chapter was worth more than a mark—the story of Noah alone, with his ark and his alcohol problem, all of it narrated by a woodworm.

Firmly determined to take my book home with her, the woman watched me. What did she want? For five minutes she'd been standing there in her brown corduroy sack coat with its thinning elbows, an open umbrella (with the slogan of a party I'd never vote for on it) in one hand; in the other, my book. Originally I wanted two marks; after tenacious haggling she had gotten me down to one. A miserable mark for a terrific piece of postmodern English literature. The woman was barely twenty. What did *she* know?

"I'm sorry, it's not for sale."

I gave her money back, which I'd been holding in my hand. Shaking her head, she loosed her talons from her prey and beat a retreat.

"Ben, can I have a word with you?" Paula asked.

I didn't trust myself to look at her, and pulled a clear plastic sheet over my books. The rain was getting heavy again.

"It doesn't work that way, Ben."

"The flea market was your idea," I said in my defense, and shot an evil eye at an old man in a raincoat trying to press some keys on my dusty old typewriter. "But apparently Berliners aren't prepared to pay modest prices for good items."

"And you're not prepared to throw anything away," Paula said, and pinched the back of my right ear, which is somewhat too big. The Raincoat Man backed off from my typewriter and looked at Paula curiously.

"And you also can't take all your junk along with you to Adam," she said. "So sell what you can. We'll throw the rest away."

My eyes roved from right to left over our stand. Next to some empty flower boxes stood two huge cartons of books from which barely one had yet been sold (and we'd been there over two hours already). Between them and my colorful collection of espresso cups, I could see a round ashtray made of red glass. It was from when I still smoked. Soon I wouldn't need it at all anymore, not even for guests.

A great gap yawned between the cups and a carton of school-books; this morning a toy castle had stood there, but only for a few minutes. It was bought for eight marks by a young couple pushing a stroller with a blissfully sleeping child in it. The castle was the only thing there that had belonged to Paula, or rather, to her son Konrad, who already considered himself too old to be playing with toy knights (he was seven).

Then, further to the left, was the old typewriter (Raincoat Man had disappeared without asking about the price) and my collection of Lorenzo Lamas posters from the 80s (many in which his delectable chest was bared, as well as a signed one my American pen pal

Hope had sent me that showed him with the rest of the *Falcon Crest* cast).

"I can't possibly throw that away," I had said to Paula when we were cleaning out the basement and she came upon this extremely valuable collection.

"If nobody buys it, you'll *have* to throw it away! Or give it away to someone," came the answer from the woman who was my best friend but had no heart.

In the shadow of the collection lay a lemon squeezer in gaudy orange. It came from my dearly beloved mother, and had served so well at so many orgies with Paula and our friend Martina as to bring me nearly to the brink of carpal tunnel syndrome. (Martina was our pet name for our favorite drink.)

"So, either you go home and let me sell your stuff alone—and at my prices—or we're both going," Paula said. "Or you can pull yourself together."

At the end of our booth was a clothes rack on which hung a suede winter coat with a fur collar (which I wouldn't need anymore once I was sucking up martinis under the palms with Adam). Leaning against the base of the rack was a pair of inline skates that I had just bought the previous summer but had banished to the closet after one wearing (I hate sports). And not to be forgotten: a tasteless Kandinsky (I hate costume jewelry and sports) that Poor Dull Daniel had given me for our second anniversary. In the upper left-hand corner was a large black circle, like the sun; on the lower right, something that looked like a deck chair that someone had tried unsuccessfully to open. After we broke up, the picture lay in the basement for months; now it was standing here in the rain. I hadn't even dusted it.

"You want another coffee?" she asked just as I was contemplating a particularly dazzling image from my Lorenzo Lamas collection: He was standing by a swimming pool in a tight, wet, white T-shirt, the water dripping from his thick chest hair, and the poster was quite damp from the steady Berlin drizzle.

I nodded sadly. Making coffee wasn't one of Paula's strengths, but you could warm your hands on the mug.

"Okay," I said. "I promise I'll be a big boy from now on."

As the steaming brown swill poured from the thermos into my plastic mug, Paula looked up suddenly and indicated something behind me with a nod of her head.

"Customer," she said, and nearly burnt my fingers as the hot coffee ran over the rim of my mug.

I took the mug in my other hand and licked my wounds as I turned around. Before me stood the woman with the worn-out corduroy sack coat and black umbrella.

"I'll take the book for fifty cents now," she said.

CHAPTER 1

Keep your distance from men who are constantly talking,
above all:
—if the talking doesn't include compliments to you
—if they suddenly take off their shirt
—if they don't have hair on their chest

Los Angeles is a bit the way I used to be when I'd be out partying:
there's just no end to it. The city is huge, not like Berlin, more like
if Berlin and Brandenburg were combined. (Because of this, it's not
enough for its millions of gays to have just one Christopher Street
Day; so there's also one for Black Pride and, in the beginning of
August, one for the city's numerous Latinos.)

In this incredibly huge city, it can take you roughly two to three
hours to get from one end of it to another (and, as is well known,
you're also not allowed to drive insanely fast). So going out always
has the sense of an excursion. Anyone with a shred of self-esteem
will start with dinner up in Malibu; then (after a forty-minute drive)
have a couple drinks at a nice bar in West Hollywood (and run into
some friends there from Burbank, who need about half an hour to
get there); at the bar you all decide to go to a cool party in Silverlake
in East Los Angeles, another half hour on the road (the traffic on
Sunset Boulevard permitting and if Santa Monica Boulevard isn't
partially blocked again for a film shoot).

In L.A. you spend about as much time in your car as Berliners
spend in the subway. And you accept this because, for one, you have

no other choice; secondly, gas there is insanely cheap (it's the same with alcohol); and so, thirdly, it doesn't matter if the next bar is only two blocks away—you take your car.

I liked Los Angeles, and even after everything that happened, I still like the city. Arriving at the airport, I had to wait for my luggage way too long, as always. Around me stood a dozen or so passengers from the same flight. The chatty French guy who was visiting his great-aunt on his father's side for the first time, and had smuggled two bottles of her favorite cognac into the country for her, was talking to an elderly English woman in tweed and acting as if he didn't want to see me, even though on the plane he had shared with me every detail of his family history.

"She'll disinherit me if those bottles are broken. If these Americans play rugby with my suitcase, I'm done for." The rich aunt was eighty-seven, was named Antonia, and emigrated with her parents after the Second World War. At that time her father was still dealing in …

Information that nobody needed from a seatmate no one wanted. On the plane I alternately feigned being asleep or simply obtuse, pulled on my headphones and turned on the Three Tenors channel and looked out the window for a long time. A very long time.

Sometimes you could see the Atlantic through a break in the clouds.

I could hardly wait to see Adam again in a few hours. Hopefully we'd land on time. He hated being kept waiting.

My Sweetie was probably cleaning the apartment one more time or preparing something to eat. When he was through with that, he'd tidy up. Every time I visited, he'd proudly introduce his newest system. The last time he had organized his socks by color (the black and navy blue ones for work had a separate drawer, as did the white ones he wore jogging—in a tray below). Perhaps at this very moment he was arranging the depths of the refrigerator by color or in alphabetical order. The first quarrel had already been preprogrammed, at the very least after two days because, "lost in thought," I would put the fat-free milk in the door of the refrigerator next to the peanut butter (which I liked just as little, and which had its place in the refrigerator by all the other yellow and ocher shades) and not in its designated place by the mozzarella cheese on the top shelf.

At the end of a particularly smarmy aria, my French seatmate burbled once more into my consciousness.

"… was still incredibly expensive at that time. So my father, the old warhorse, used a trick. See, his cousin was there …"

Only when we got our meal and, out of sheer despair, I spilled a glass of red wine on his ridiculous floral shirt (apparently he was flying on to Hawaii), did I get not only some rest but also more room. He spent the rest of the flight in his undershirt in a seat farther up.

Now I looked on with envy as he lugged a scruffy brown leather suitcase off the conveyor belt, loaded it on his luggage trolley, and shoved off.

A gray box with "Fragile" written on it was going past me for the thirty-seventh time, but still there wasn't a trace of my luggage.

As always.

This conspiracy against poor little me has been going on for years now. It began in London, when I was twenty-two, on my very first flight. But I didn't become suspicious of anything till much later. But the conspirators are everywhere, in every corner of this godforsaken earth. They must have bugged the booking system, a perfect ruse. They're informed of my every step: where and how long I stay anywhere, to the minute. The swine even played their rotten little game in Thailand when I was there with Poor Dull Daniel.

I took off my coat and looked around. Harmless people, beyond whom there was no one. The woman in the floral-print summer dress and flip-flops was on her cell phone non-stop, as she had been ever since the "Fasten Seatbelt" light had gone off. Diagonally behind her I spotted the fat guy who had occupied one and a half seats (his little daughter crammed in next to him); he passed the time with only two bananas, but certainly wouldn't be waiting to eat much longer.

Friends have sometimes claimed that they too have felt hounded (or maybe better here: impounded?) at times, but these were just shoddy attempts to calm me down. I saw through all of them.

Even Daniel tried telling me the whole thing was a coincidence, and that I had an overactive imagination.

"Grow up!" he hissed, rolling his eyes—a typical comment from a bore.

Meanwhile I could imagine their ugly mugs quite clearly. They always come in pairs and they're always the same types: A short, fat one and a tall, angular one with an overbite. The fat one knocks out the driver; the tall one goes through the luggage. It all has to happen quickly, so nobody else notices.

Finally the thin one finds what he's looking for. He holds the straps of the suitcase between his thick fingers and grins with leering satisfaction.

"Ben Sandlot, we got you again," he mutters, the stump of a cigarette smoldering at the left corner of his mouth.

As the other suitcases on the conveyor belt disappear, one after the other, through the hatch to the pickup area, he hauls mine to the side and sets his skinny ass on it. He pulls out a new cigarette and laughs this horrible laugh that drones all the way inside to the luggage carousel. (Of course Poor Dull Daniel always claimed he never heard it.) Sometimes it's six or seven cigarettes till the last baggage carrier is unloaded and my suitcase is finally released.

So today again I stood at the conveyor belt like an idiot to the bitter end (at any rate, I have the best story of all of them). I had already stashed my bulky army rucksack on the luggage trolley (they usually let one piece of my luggage come through right away to lure me into a false sense of security), but my suitcase was nowhere to be seen.

I pulled my wallet out of my pocket and looked at the photo Paula had slipped to me at the airport before my flight. A self-portrait, nude, on her guest couch.

"Yours always," she had written on her left leg with a black Sharpie.

"By that I mean the couch and me. You can come back whenever you want and sleep on the couch. It's all yours."

The last few days before I left, I lived with Paula and her son Konrad.

We had known each other since kindergarten, had exchanged clothes with each other, and for years couldn't let an afternoon or evening pass without seeing each other. Yet I had never seen Paula naked.

Not that it would have excited me.

"I know, dumbass," Paula said. "but I thought it'd be a clever way to keep you from forgetting me too fast. You're going to miss me."

How could I ever forget her! Paula makes the worst coffee you can imagine, but she's my best friend—apart from her part-time job as mother-, sister- and older brother-substitute. She always protected me at school when the boys from the upper grades wanted to beat me up.

"Go play some soccer, or at least pick on someone who can fight—and keep your testosterone level under control."

Then they were stumped for a while: they had to go look up "testosterone" in the dictionary.

Paula kissed me on the mouth, turned around, and left me standing at the security check-in. I watched her as she pulled that atrocious yellow-green crocheted cap over her short brown hair until the escalator carried her from view. She vanished, without even turning around once.

The conveyor belt was clearly emptier; even the box with the fragile contents was gone.

As I lifted my left arm to check my watch, I surmised that a shower would be a good thing for all involved.

Local time was 6:47 p.m.

We had landed thirty minutes late. So Adam had already been waiting for me over an hour. The roses he had brought along would surely have wilted long ago. The bouquet, a massive thing, is now a sorry sight: The leaves fall one after another to the floor. My Sweetie had held it bravely to his chest (the hair on which is in the attractive manner of Lorenzo Lamas) and glared and waited and glared and got impatient simply because his Little Guy wasn't turning the corner with his luggage trolley and bags. Couldn't he just be on time for once?

I thought I'd give him the reunion present later, at home, in the apartment: a pair of dark blue, sexy shorts, from which the treasure trail just below the navel (which in Adam's case was like a six-lane freeway) could temptingly push. First we'd have long, filthy sex, and when I recovered, I'd crawl to my suitcase and—

The conveyor belt was nearly empty; a lone plaid canvas suitcase was making its fifth victory lap alongside a dark blue umbrella. (An American pop song once claimed that it never rains in Southern California, and the tourism industry is wary of contradicting it.)

So there I stood, all alone. Maybe my suitcase with the sexy shorts in it never left the airport in Berlin, or had ended up in godforsaken Kristnestad. (Is there even an airport in Kristinestad?)

I looked at my watch.

By now the roses had lost all their leaves and lay trampled on the floor. Adam had hurled them there in anger, stomped all over them, and was now sitting, his arms folded, in one of those plastic chairs, perhaps had even fallen asleep. Security people were skulking around him, eying him suspiciously. What was this guy waiting for? Did someone forget him here? Abandon him? Was he even still breathing? That'd be awful … No, look: his chest is moving up and down—Ewwww! Is that hair sticking out from the collar of his shirt?!

This is Los Angeles, California, where a young woman gets breast enlargement as a gift for her eighteenth birthday, and a young man gets his chest waxed. Where there are basically three archenemies: age, cigarettes, and body hair. Where the locals on the beach ask you inquisitively which planet you come from when they see that you haven't cropped your chest hair to within a quarter of an inch or, better yet, had it removed entirely..

On a digital ad on Santa Monica Boulevard, one of the most-traveled streets in Los Angeles, you can read how many people have died so far in the past year from nicotine-related causes. Yet the number of those who have bled to death from armpit-, chest-, leg- and toe-shaving goes unrecorded. That's California censorship.

All the same, it wasn't the people's here fault: it was the other people who had elected George W. Bush.

At the beginning of 2001, one believed the new president capable of anything: insane rearmament, perhaps abolishing the State Department, or driving climate policy back to the Middle Ages. You graciously assumed that the Texan was capable of nibbling on a pretzel without choking on it and flopping off the couch. How one would later marvel (and bitch).

Personally, I prefer a president who gets nibbled on by interns and gets their dresses all messy.

Which is still far better than having absolutely nothing to wear.

The British Airways people couldn't explain themselves or the loss of my suitcase, so they did what they do second-best: Apologize.

"So you don't think it's possible, Mr. Sandlot, that someone might have picked it up by mistake? Perhaps there was a mix-up."

"Fine," I said. "But then there should still be a yellow hard-shell suitcase around, right?" (One that looked like mine but contained secret government documents or maybe Mrs. Van Hoskins' jewelry, like in that movie with Ryan O'Neal and Barbra Streisand.)

Without a word, I took the care package for stranded passengers and towed my rucksack to the arrival hall. Hopefully they hadn't arrested Adam for unauthorized hanging out and cleared him out like a suspicious package or bag—or, not even to be imagined: defused him!

Through the window over the exit I could see the first palm trees. Beyond the treetops, which towered over the parking garage across the way, was that impeccable blue sky that never gets dull and always makes you feel like you're on vacation. Los Angeles doesn't have many places of interest, but nothing can top that sky.

The crowd of people waiting for arriving passengers came clearly into view. A large Japanese family celebrated the arrival of one its members with colorful balloons and kitschy songs. One of them held up a banner that I couldn't read; another, probably the father, took a picture of his family with the balloons and banner.

Behind them stood a young couple who were intensely investigating whether they had forgotten how to kiss since they last saw each other. (I kept looking over at them. They were making out for a pretty long time. Is that a good sign or a bad sign?)

I became aware of a dull feeling in my stomach. What if all of a sudden I didn't care if Adam tried on his new shorts (assuming no one at the Kristinestad airport had any use for them), and even less whether he ever took them off?

What if we were just with each other by rote. If our paths parted again after, at the very latest, two weeks, and I flew back to Germany and he went on with his life here?

If watching *Who Wants to Be a Millionaire?* would eventually become our leisure activity of choice.

"And now the $10,000 question: Which American president, upon arrival at the Kristinestad airport in 1951, bemoaned the loss of a bright yellow hard-shell suitcase and postponed a summit meeting with the Finnish prime minister at the time, Urho Kekkonen, to get a different gift for his host?

    a) Richard Nixon
    b) Theodore Roosevelt
    c) Harry Truman
    d) John F. Kennedy
    or
    e) Jimmy Carter."

We had last seen each other three months ago; now, right before our reunion, wasn't exactly the best time for doubts. I had nine hours for them during the flight. I could've used my last night with Paula to let her proofread my thoughts.

No, I had to wait until I was in the Los Angeles airport to start up with this stuff, on the very first day of my new life with Adam, a life that I'd dreamt about for two years,

"Okay, I'll take the question back. But instead answer this: Which four of these seven things about Adam do you love the most:

His little ears.
His smell when he comes back from jogging.
His decisiveness and assertiveness.
The precision and speed of his fingers when slicing onions.
The hair on his chest.
The hair on his underarms.
The hair on his toes."

CHAPTER 2

You shouldn't talk to strangers,
especially if they:
—aren't witty
—try to be witty, and
—fail utterly

I had met Adam on vacation two years ago.

We lay around a lot, lazy and hip, at Venice Beach, and drank red wine from a soda bottle we had filled, so we wouldn't be accused of tempting the under-agers with the pleasures of alcohol.

In the distance you could hear the 70s disco grooves a black DJ was laying down for a group of inline skaters, who were moving to the beat. Around us lay couples and families in swimming suits and shorts beneath big, brightly colored umbrellas shielding them against the sun. A woman with remarkably beautiful breasts (that certainly weren't cheap), refreshed herself by rubbing a cold water bottle up and down her arms.

Adam was wearing a sweater, long pants and thick socks in black dress shoes. We'd been lying there for an hour, and he had sweat on his brow—a great mystery to me.

"Not that I'm complaining," I said as I knocked the sand off my jeans and rolled up my sleeves, which were always sliding back down over my elbows, "but it's pretty warm today."

How I'd have loved to have seen that carpet of hair he was concealing beneath his sweater, small spurs of which had forged their way over the collar into the outer world, whetting one's appetite like the headline to an enthralling story.

Adam sat up and looked at me.

"You wanna go somewhere inside and get something cold to drink?"

I didn't dare expose any of my body parts because I didn't want him to feel pressured to do the same, and, even less, give him the impression that I couldn't wait for our relationship to become physical.

Also, I was afraid that a confrontation with my rather un-Californian body would have an immediate and detrimental effect on our relationship ever getting physical. Ever since grade school I've been allergic to wrestling mats, chin-up bars, and cinder tracks. No one would ever catch me at a gym unless it served smart martinis.

"Sure. I'm also starting to get hungry. Maybe we can get something to eat."

"Why don't we just go back to my apartment? I've got a bunch of stuff in the fridge."

Adam stood up and took a couple steps back. Then he stuck his hands so deep in his pockets you expected them to reappear at the end of his pants legs, shrugged his shoulders, and gave his boyish grin.

"I'd also just really like to cook something for you, little guy."

As long as I've been thinking—and I started thinking particularly early, often, and avidly about men—there have been two ways for a guy to win me over: when he cooks for me (even if it's just water for the hot-water bottle); and when he calls me "little guy". And it doesn't even matter if I'm actually—as in this case—about half an inch taller than him. Since suddenly I had an urgent need for our relationship to become physical, I agreed to go.

On the way there, I heard this song for the first time on KBIG 104, sung by a warm, clear, female voice …

Why do birds suddenly appear
Every time you are near?
Just like me, they long to be
Close to you.
Why do stars fall down fr—

Adam changed the station.

"Hey, what was that?" I asked.

The song had obviously been recorded in the 70s, and I asked myself why it would take someone twenty-nine years to finally come across it.

"Why do you want to know?"

He looked at me as if I had said something horrifically idiotic.

"Maybe because it's one of the prettiest songs I've ever heard?"

"The Carpenters," he answered grudgingly. "I had a cassette of theirs when I was a kid. Horrific."

"Had?"

Admittedly, I had considered the Carpenters a folk-rock band whose music best lent itself to wearing plaid shirts and chopping down trees in the forest. But now I had the urge to *plant* trees or to put buttercups in my hair.

"Forget it. Even if I knew where it was, I wouldn't give it to you."

Adam wasn't exactly the romantic type, but that didn't bother me. I was romantic enough on my own.

It took him an hour to make the food. I gazed at him, full of wonder, as he carefully cleaned the zucchini and carved it into uniformly sized slices. I, however, was driven to despair when I couldn't open a package of pasta quickly enough.

There was chicken with Red Hot Chili Peppers—the only music we could agree on.

Afterwards neither of us wanted to move for a while, and we dropped onto the couch with full stomachs—where we soon found a type of movement that was accommodating to us both, in horny anticipation of which I hadn't jacked in three days.

As is generally known, the term "same-sex love" refers to the practice of getting samely sexual with each other right away, and so I was proud at the time that I had known Adam a couple days already before we did it the first time.

As I said, this guy was a walking carpet sample, and I don't mean a couple hairs on the left, a couple on the right, and maybe three more between his navel and his pleasure center, I mean: *really hairy*. The fleeciest hair you could want. And what the critics refuse to believe: Underneath it you find everything you need.

"Promise me you'll never go California Razor Crazy on me," I whispered, and fiddled with his nipples.

"You don't think I'm a hairy ape?"

He winked his left eye.

Hairy ape? That would have to be the official discriminatory term in California for someone defiantly anti-razor.

By way of answer, I kissed the hair on his big toe.

We don't go right home from the airport.

After we've left the freeway, Adam turns left instead of right onto Santa Monica Boulevard in the direction of the beach.

The whole way there I'm rubbing the back of his head, sometimes touching his small ears quite by accident.

I tell him about my going-away party at the editorial office, how Carstensen had to be carried to a cab because he couldn't walk anymore. Proudly report how I got rid of my winter coat for fifty marks at the flea market. Say nothing about not a single buyer taking a liking to my Lorenzo Lamas collection, and how I managed to persuade Paula to keep the pictures for me. Show him the nude photo. Give him her regards, which he's happy about. He gives me a hello from his best friend Brenda.

"Wow!" I say. "I'm finally here now, and don't have to go back again in two weeks. Ain't that gorgeous?"

When we get to the beach, we nestle next to each other and stare at the ocean; the sun is sinking lower every moment.

Adam strokes my hair, and sings my favorite song into my ear …

That is why all the girls in town
Follow you all around
Just like me they long to be
Close to you

This was pretty much how I had pictured my arrival in Los Angeles to be.

I grabbed my shoe from next to the foot of the bed and slammed it on the clock radio on the nightstand. The channel, an oldies station, jumped; the Carpenters fell silent and instead a loud hissing filled the room. I sat up and turned off the radio.

3:27. Middle of the night, and outside the window was blackest night. And Adam had to be out there somewhere.

I waited two hours at the airport; he didn't come.

I phoned all the hospitals in the area, went to the police. His answering machine wouldn't take messages anymore after the third time I tried reaching him at home. He seemed to be saying, "Leave me out of the story!" and then tossing me off the line after the greeting message.

Adam's cell only offered an interminable dial tone. Maybe he had lost it somewhere.

Or had his bank been robbed and he lay tied up and alone on some cold basement floor. An ugly black piece of tape over that beautiful mouth? He tried to call out every time the phone rang, but no one could hear him. Next to him was the safe, wide open and cleaned out; the thieves had only left a bundle of five dollar notes behind—and a horrible mess. Adam must have felt awful. What was interesting, though, was that it wasn't reported at all in the news; there was nothing suspicious going on in front of the bank when I drove by. No police; no broadcast vans for all the local TV stations.

Then I sat for a few hours in front of his apartment. His neighbor, a sweet old lady with fake hair, had let me in and, after the first hour, brought me a cup of tea.

We sat there a while together.

"He's a good boy, always friendly. No loud parties, no women visitors after 10:00. Where do you know him from?"

Actually, Adam was one of those guy you could picture having women visitors, which made him all the more appealing.

"And you don't know when the last time you saw him was?" I asked for the tenth time, and the question always made as little sense, since I'd just spoken with him on the phone the night before my flight.

"I don't go out much. And I don't hear all that well anymore. But wait a minute: No, it has to be over a week."

She saw the disappointment in my face.

"But I'm sure you must have just missed each other at the airport. And now he's angry and sitting in a bar somewhere having a drink. Believe me, my husband did it all the time when I'd stay out with my girlfriends longer than he liked. To tell the truth, he did it one too many times. It got so I'd throw him out when he came home drunk."

Should her stories have encouraged me, or was she just inciting me to mischief? I wasn't sure. Waiting wasn't my strength, and so I wrote Adam a short note that I shoved under the door and wished the old lady good night.

I found a hotel downtown (it was five listenings of "Close to You" away from Adam's apartment). The elevator was broken; the window in my room wouldn't open. It smelled like a mixture of cigarette smoke and socks that someone had worn for five days straight and then left in the room. But I could tolerate it for a night. Early tomorrow morning I'd get the redemptive call from Adam, and a few minutes later he'd be standing in the lobby to pick me up and carry my rucksack.

I couldn't reach Paula. She must have been out somewhere, picking up Konrad from school.

I left her a message with the number of the hotel.

I dialed Adam's cell number for the thirtieth time. It rang for so long that I thought I was hearing his phone ring in the next room. Nothing happened—and then:

"Hello?"

I was so surprised that I forgot to say anything.

"Hello. Who is this?"

It was a woman's voice. I had misdialed.

I got up from the bed and tried to open the window again. Useless. I leaned my forehead against the pane of glass.

Across the street I spotted an old theater. It looked run-down, and the lettering was weathered.

The first time I came to Los Angeles as Adam's lover and Poor Dull Daniel's ex, we saw a play down in West Hollywood by a very hip American playwright. It was about Maria Callas, and she was played by a way-too-fat and way-too-gay man. It was awful, but Adam and I had a wonderful day behind us and nothing could destroy our mood.

As we entered the theater, he ran down to the front row with our tickets and claimed that people were sitting in our seats. The people, a young couple with identical glasses, were upset and apologized profusely. They got up and caused such a bother that even people in the second row got up, and were still figuring out their seats when the play began, while we had long ago taken seats in the fifth row and my ears of different size were glowing with admiration for Adam. That was when I started planning my move to America and further steps.

"Ladies and gentlemen, could I please have your attention for a moment? No, that wasn't from the play, and I'm certainly no actor. Excuse me, I'll sit back down in a second. I just have to—Yes, I'll be quick. Adam, can you see me? I'm up here.—Will you marry me?"

I had fallen asleep for a few minutes when the telephone rang.

"Ben, where are you? What's going on? Did you two have a fight? Did you get bitchy again?"

Typical Paula.

"We didn't have a chance to fight."

I had to yawn. I was getting lightheaded.

"Did he meet someone?"

"Something's happened to Adam, Paula. He wasn't at the airport. He's not at his apartment. His answering machine is full because he hasn't checked it in days. His neighbor hasn't seen him for a long time. Nobody knows where he is."

"You just talked to him the day before yesterday."

"I've asked at the hospitals. Next I'm going to call his bank, but I'm afraid he's not there either."

"There's got to be a perfectly reasonable explanation. Maybe the two of you just somehow missed each other at the airport. Did you land on time?""

"No, but that's not my fault."

Suddenly I thought of my suitcase. I had given them Adam's address. When they can't deliver it there, they'll probably send it back again.

"Maybe he was at the wrong terminal. Maybe he got the day wrong, or the time. Or he got stuck in traffic. So many things might've happened," Paula said.

"I just feel really shitty."

"That's not surprising, since you've been on your feet for twenty-four hours. You're kicking off a new life, and it's had a rotten start. It can only get better."

"That was my motto when I decided to leave Berlin," I said.

"And be glad you did. It hasn't stopped raining here a second since you left. It was the right decision."

"Okay," I said. "I promise to be a big boy from now on."

"And if it just doesn't work out with you two, you know: my couch ..."

"I know: your couch."

I looked at the photo of her.

"Paula, has anybody ever told you that you have uncannily beautiful breasts?"

I could hear her trying to suppress a laugh on her end of the line.

"I didn't give you that picture so you could make fun of me."

"Thanks so much, sweet stuff. Wish you were here."

Before I went back to sleep, I called around again to all the big hospitals. To no effect.

Then I tried reaching Adam at home. Now his answering machine didn't even pick up.

A soft knock at the door wakes me up.

When I open the door, I don't see anyone.

It's completely dark in the hallway; muffled screams from one of the opposite rooms.

I take the elevator to the lobby, which takes an unusually long time. No one is at the reception desk. No one appears, even though

I'm standing there at least ten minutes. I sit in the bar, listen to sub-dued piano music and order a Cosmo.

In the corner there's a piano that no one's playing.

A young bellboy enters the bar wearing nothing but a pair of un-derwear. He's holding a sign with my name on it at his chest.

I follow him.

We walk through the lobby, where I spot Paula. She's sitting on my suitcase, completely nude, but she can't see me.

I follow the bellboy up to the roof of the hotel, where there's an enormous swimming pool without water in it. At the end of the pool there's a diving platform.

Adam is sitting way up, on the ten-meter board, and waves to me. I want to climb up, but the ladder is blocked. I wave back to him and make signs that he should come down to me. Adam stands up and jumps.

My own scream wakes me up.

It was a little before 7:00, the sun was already up. My head hurt and I was dizzy. I went to the bathroom, thought about the bellboy in Adam's undies and jacked off. Then I had a drink of water and went back to bed.

I missed Adam, and it was worse than when I was in Germany. When I missed him there, I knew he was far away. The good thing about a long-distance relationship with a time difference is that, when you can't sleep at night, you can call the other guy without feeling guilty about having woken him up just to let him know you can't sleep.

Now I was in his city, and he seemed farther away than before.

It was seven that night when I finally woke from my coma.

No one had called, or I hadn't heard it.

It was too late to call his bank, so I wanted to try his house again. Then I noticed that the receiver wasn't placed right in the cradle.

I asked at the reception desk whether any messages had been left for me. Nothing.

My head was still hurting. I took a cold shower to wake up.

Then I tried Adam's number again, but hung up after the second ring. Then I ordered a taxi at the reception desk.

The Abbey is one of the nicest bars in West Hollywood, and one of the gayest—a rare combination. A martini (or, what passes for one in America; it comes in twenty-seven different flavors, and has little to do with the usual German dosage or with just adding lemon juice or a slice) costs as much as a weekly subway pass in Berlin, and you can sit or stand outside there all year long, day and night. The overhead heat lamps keep you from freezing, and you feel like you're getting drunk quicker.

On the weekends, a DJ plays good house music, and you feel like you're at a garden party with rich friends who have acquired their wealth by doing business with overpriced martinis.

Inside, a cozy electric fire is burning in the fireplace, and groups of three or four people can go off into the cabanas or lounge about in brown leather play areas. In the bathroom there are all sorts of colognes and lollipops, and an attentive Mexican man who gives you a towel after you've washed your hands in the hope you'll hand him a dollar after you've dried them.

The Abbey is on a side street off Santa Monica Boulevard, in a part of West Hollywood that's so gay the crosswalks are considered runways, since you're always being watched by at least two cars when you cross the street (that is, if they let you). Sometimes, if you're in your car, right at the front by the runway, you can influence the movements of the models as they cross the street (if you let them) by turning up your music really loud.

In statistical terms, compared with the rest of Los Angeles, here you have the best chance of getting across the street unscathed.

But the deciding factor isn't the good will of the drivers, but the good looks of the pedestrians.

It was a wonderful, warm evening, the air still heated from the day. You could see every single star in the sky.

Then all of a sudden I noticed Adam, his small ears and his pitch-black hair, which had seen thicker days. (The guys in Berlin simply shave their head at the first sign of anything falling out; I couldn't even look at all those baldies anymore.)

It was in the Abbey; he was standing in a group of guys a few yards away from the DJ. A scrawny kid, twenty at the most, a backwards-baseball-cap type, was resting his arm on Adam's shoulder, laughing his not-even-twenty-yet laugh. I was standing too far away to see where Adam's hand was, and I didn't want to risk being seen.

The two of them were constantly whispering to each other, and Adam was clearly luxuriating in the attention of the minor in the baseball cap, who undoubtedly didn't appreciate a single word Adam was saying and really just wanted to get at those sweet ears.

The other three in the circle were mere sycophants, content to bask in Adam's radiance, and who, at unobserved moments, whispered to one another about what a cute couple the two made, Adam and the dumb baseball cap. They didn't have the slightest idea. God, I felt such pitty for them.

I got an apple martini at the bar, and took up my observation post again.

I was nervous. What could I say to Adam? Should I even say anything at all? And if I so, should I say it in front of his weird friends?

It has to be something, I thought, that he won't soon forget— and that horrible thing hanging around his neck, even less soon. This was the goal I set myself, perhaps an unnecessarily difficult project.

At any rate, the two customary California come-ons— "Yahavinfun?" and "Howarya?"—were ruled out.

"I like your ears" was certainly original, but maybe somewhat confusing.

Or what about: "I think it's just smokin' hot the way your hair's thinning in the front. I hope you're not taking anything to stop it."

At another time this could be a nice compliment, but as the lead-in to a rapprochement?

"Surely it's time for your little friend to go to bed, and then maybe you'd like to talk about something that's actually interesting."

This wasn't so terribly evil, but the woman with the fondness for ugly crocheted caps always said that the period for eliminating the weak spots in the other guy's circle of friends didn't begin until you had made yourself irreplaceable, that is, about three or four months into a relationship.

"Where're you from?" asked someone off to my right. A big muscle guy in a wife-beater, knee-length white shorts and red sneakers ginned at me.

I shrugged, and just about dislocated my neck trying to hold Adam in my line of vision.

"Was I thinking out loud again? That's pretty nuts, huh?"

He laughed and shook his head.

"No, it's actually totally adorable."

Help! You can't calmly plan how to get the most attractive guy of the evening without getting hit on by the second most attractive.

"Luckily you couldn't hear what I was saying."

"I'm sure nothing bad could have come out of a pretty mouth like that."

The muscle guy had just been catapulted from the list of the Top Ten Most Attractive.

I grimaced by way of answer.

"Believe me, I was debating whether in my battle for the best guy of the night I should first tar and feather my rival, or if I had the time to do some stretch exercises with him."

"Definitely the tar and feathers—it's almost impossible to get the feathers off afterwards."

Oh how badly the muscle guy wanted to get back on the list.

"Thanks a lot, that's a good argument for proceeding as planned."

To be particularly impolite, I took a couple steps away from him, mainly because I wanted to see what my beloved was doing, only to discover that he had vanished with all of his fake friends.

It was a bad start. I had to wait nearly a week and invest a good deal of my vacation money in expensive drinks until I saw Adam again.

I found myself again at the place where I'd first spotted Adam's small ears a year and a half ago, but this time with little spirit at all.

The Abbey was so full you'd have thought they were giving supersaver offers on martinis. Trying to make one's way through the crowd, you inevitably stepped on someone's foot or knocked into someone (which in California was considered a conversation-starter; mean looks were for the East Coast or Germany).

The DJ was pounding the crowd with sugary sweet Janet Jackson platitudes. I was on the lookout for Adam's friends, for people we'd met at parties; people who might have seen him or who knew how he was, or knew the name of the guy he'd been seen with a lot lately ("He's no competition for you, sweetie!") and where the little trollop lived.

Adam wasn't at home. Where else should I look for him?

A circuit past the dessert bar, the cabanas, and back to the bar proved fruitless. I felt like someone was watching me intently, but when I turned around, I didn't see anything suspicious. Maybe I had imagined it.

I left the Abbey. But even in all the clubs and bars around the corner on Santa Monica Boulevard I couldn't spot a remotely familiar face.

I hated nothing more than to have to go to these places alone, and missed Adam something awful. It never bothered him to lead the way; I usually followed him at about a half a yard's distance so I could watch the greedy looks he drew as he walked by, and smiled my soft, understanding, and somewhat proud smile.

I had a beer at the last club and called the search off for the day. It was one of these places that plays chintzy top-40 stuff. For one or two dollars you could grab a stripper between the legs or on the ass, and could be groped yourself at any time without financial compensation. Maybe they shouldn't have abolished backrooms in this country.

Adam and I had hooked up here two, maybe three times. One of the faces behind the bar looked familiar to me: a big sweet lunk with glasses and extremely thick pecs, who upstairs worked naked but downstairs in floral pants like the ones Paula wears to bed.

I took my glass of beer to the darkest corner of the place so I wouldn't have to talk to anyone, and watched the videos playing on monitors above the dance floor.

It hadn't been two minutes when this guy, who on a Walk-Past Scale of one-to-ten was a 7.9, emerged from an even darker corner and pushed so closely past me that his hand accidentally grazed my stomach. Then he disappeared in the bathroom. A little later he came back and stood next to me.

"Hi."

I just kept watching the monitors and said nothing back.

"You here alone?"

"No," I lied.

"I am."

I took a big gulp of my beer, and looked at my watch.

"Gotta go already? Where're your friends? Someone like you has gotta have a lot of hot friends."

If there's anything I hate, it's guys who stick their tongue in my ear (either one) because they're afraid that their extremely important pronouncements might fall victim to the loud music.

I moved away a step from the 8.4, had another big swallow of my beer, and took a longer look at my watch.

"You dominant?"

I tried to be semi-friendly when I looked at him, but found immediately that the corners of my mouth were following gravity and not my good intentions.

"Lemme just have my beer in quiet, okay?"

Now, apparently in Los Angeles there were several competing ideas about what having a beer in quiet meant. He pushed his hand between my legs and whispered that he wanted to submit to me.

I dominantly threw the rest of my beer in his face, and ran out of the club.

The part with the beer isn't true. But on the way to the hotel I wished so badly I had done it, since I had forgotten out of sheer surprise to yell at the guy. For a second I even thought of turning and hitting him. I went by foot, running through Los Angles in the middle of the night in the direction of the hotel.

When I finally got there after an hour, the lady at the reception desk called to me. She regarded me with tiny, tired eyes.

"Hang on a minute. A fax came for you."

CHAPTER 3

You have to be ready to forgive the other guy, if:
—he has a good explanation
—he begs you on his knees for forgiveness
—as long as he's kneeling…

It was all just a big mistake.

Adam is sitting in front of me, and is crying like I've never seen anyone cry before. He fends off all my attempts to calm him.

While he's talking, his eyes dart back and forth, always avoiding me. He has dark circles under his eyes, he hasn't shaved in days, and it smells musty in his apartment, as if he hasn't left it in a long time and not opened the windows. The smell in my hotel is nothing compared to it.

"I don't know if I can be with you, and I'd understand if you got up and left … I've met someone; we've slept together a few times."

He wipes tears off his face and looks to the floor.

"I don't expect you to believe me, but it doesn't mean any-thing—not about you and me. I've been thinking about us the past few hours, and I don't want to live without you, little guy. I love you."

And then: Great wailing on both sides; wild embracing; nasty making out; endless fucking, and blissful sleep.

That was one of the more tenacious scenarios that I pictured as I sat in my stinking hotel room. In another version Adam reports that he's had an AIDS test. He had, shortly after we first met, gone to a bath house because he missed me and having sex with me after I had left, and it must've happened this one time, otherwise he always controlled himself, and he was so sorry and he didn't want to live without me, and he loved me.

Always the same ending.

"It's all bullshit!" Paula said when she called. It was her fax that the woman at the reception desk gave me.

"WELL?"

(That's all she wrote.)

"You have to keep looking for him," she said.

"Why isn't *he* looking for *me*? Why isn't he calling?"

"Maybe he can't."

I had given up everything for Adam: Berlin; Paula. And a steady job at the newspaper.

"Don't you want to think it over some? Take a half year's unpaid vacation. Take a whole year, for all I care."

Other than the fact that Carstensen, my boss, was always the first to be propped up dead drunk in the corner at the office Christmas party, he was a good guy. Tall, gangly, with a choleric person's early warning system: He'd scratch his beard when something with mistakes in it had gone to print, which unleashed a torrent of screaming that went on for minutes, one per forgotten comma, two for spelling mistakes ("Oh, so Petersen is a long-standing member of the *SDP*? And a close friend of Chancellor Schroooooooooder, huh? Why did anyone even send an asshole like you to school?"), and five minutes for mistakes in content.

Carstensen had gotten the idea into his head that I should put out a daily Hollywood column, and, when necessary, also report on philandering presidents and students running amok at school—stories about America people always like to read.

I accepted.

"Are you sure that you want to live in California the rest of your life?"

"Absolutely," I said.

Of course, I wasn't sure at the time, but that was my business. Apart from that, I didn't want to start my life with Adam as a half- or full-year unpaid probation period. It didn't seem fair.

Now that I was in Los Angeles, though, my concept of fairness had somewhat changed.

I cranked the window down; the sun was finally ready to go down. The palm trees that lined the street in front of Adam's house threw some welcome shade on my car. I turned the car off. I didn't need the air conditioning anymore.

He'd been home for half an hour. I had almost jumped out of the car as soon as he got home. I wanted to call his name and run to him, but something held me back.

Adam appeared to be enjoying the best of health. He wasn't on crutches, and his arm wasn't in a cast; on the contrary, he was carrying two large bags, from which protruded the necks of wine bottles. Probably he was making a tasty dinner; certainly his guest was on the way. I figured it'd be just one person: manly; young; attractive.

"If it makes you feel better, then drive there and camp out in front of his house if you have to," Paula had said. "But you won't find anything out, believe me."

It actually did feel better—in any case, better than sitting at the hotel all day trying to use supernatural powers I didn't possess to make the phone ring. I had stuck a piece of paper with a big "NO!" on it to the receiver to keep me from dialing Adam's number. Later I tore it up and called his bank. A coworker answered and I asked for Adam, but I hung up as soon as she started to put me through to him. This time I wrote the "NO!" bigger, and left the hotel to go rent a car.

Nothing was going on in front of Adam's building.

"I can't wait for you to get here, little guy. I've actually taken the first week off. Maybe we can go away somewhere for a few days. So get your sexy ass over here."

It annoyed me that remembering the sound of Adam's voice, of his heavy breathing during our last phone call, made me want to sleep with him.

I got out of the car.

It was so clean that you could use your reflection in the dark blue finish to squeeze your nastier zits. That's the good thing about rentals: You don't have to waste your time on incidentals like washing it or controlling the oil-level.

The last clean car I owned was in Berlin at the time Adam had visited me there. It was January, and you had to wear gloves—not because it was so cold, but more because you'd get your fingers filthy trying to open a door or the trunk. The perfect anti-theft system.

I was on vacation at the time, but was called personally by my boss to come to a meeting introducing a new series on the house pets of Berlin politicians. Carstensen wanted to make me project director, as I had been on the makeover campaign for a grubby section of Berlin called Wedding (my great title: "My Best Friend's Wedding"), featuring portraits of the quaint and endearing locals.

"I don't kiss as well as your American gentleman caller, Sandlot, but perhaps you can tear yourself away and honor us with your presence."

The meeting was in the middle of the day and was extremely unproductive. I left the editorial office in a worse mood than I'd had when I arrived two hours before, and waited in front of the entrance for Adam, who was supposed to pick me up. But he didn't come. A group of pubescent schoolgirls ran out giggling from between parked cars. It took a few minutes before I realized that the sparkling car in the parking spot belonged to me, and I went closer.

Adam opened the door, and was beaming even more than my new old, clean Saab.

I shut the door and leaned back against a palm tree so that I couldn't be seen from his apartment window.

The horizon was dark red; the sun was going down. A nauseating and chintzy postcard image, Adam had once deemed it, and I agreed with him, albeit begrudgingly.

I turned around as a car turned into the street. An old brown Ford; it was still too far away, and I couldn't see who was sitting at the steering wheel. It drove very slowly past Adam's building. Then the Ford passed my car, and for a second I was at eye level with the driver. It was a young woman with short hair; she grinned at me and drove on.

"Maybe you just want to get a room somewhere first, Ben. Then we can wait and see how it goes the first couple months."

"But I want to be with you."

"You can always move in with me later. Or we can look for a bigger apartment together."

But I wouldn't hear anything of the sort.

Also: why?

"If you're having second thoughts, just say so," I snapped.

"It's not that I don't want to live with you."

"But that's certainly what it sounds like!"

Paula thought that Adam had just gotten cold feet all of a sudden, and that I should just let him be for a few days, maybe then he'd calm down again. But she didn't know him as well as I did. Adam always had very clear ideas about how things should go. He had well-defined goals, and made decisions easily—which I loved a lot about him.

In the two years that we knew each other, rarely had he ever changed an opinion, not about people or things, and certainly not about music or sunsets (they were too unorderly for him). It was like you had to bring him all this evidence and only then would he slowly be swayed, provided you had given him the feeling that it would hurt you to be right.

Somewhere a car door closed. I looked over at Adam's building, but couldn't see anyone.

Suddenly I felt a hand on my shoulder.

"Ben? Is that you?"

I turned around, startled.

A woman was smiling at me. Her face looked familiar.

She hugged me and said she was sorry about everything.

"What are you doing here, Ben?"

Then it hit me. I had been at a birthday party with Adam at a huge house with a pool somewhere in the San Fernando Valley, in the less-hip northern area (if size-wise Los Angeles is comparable to a combined Berlin/Brandenburg, then the Valley is as attractive as Brandenburg).

Her name was ... Brenda.

"I'm Linda. We know each other."

She lit a cigarette somewhat clumsily.

"I'm sorry, you probably don't remember me."

"No, I do. It just took me a minute."

Brenda was early fifties with a tad too much makeup. You could read her age in the tiny lines along her upper lip, also by the tons of cigarettes she sucked on a little too frantically.

"Are you waiting for Adam? But his car's right over there."

I was at a loss for words, I felt like I'd been caught, and I was annoyed that Brenda had discovered me.

"Listen, I'm going up to him now, and ..."

As she looked for something in her purse, she gripped the cigarette with the corner of her mouth, and started nervously blinking away the smoke as it crawled into her eyes.

"If you like, give me a call. Maybe we can have something to eat together."

She gave me her card and kissed me goodbye on the cheek.

"I'm terribly sorry, love. Gimme a call, huh?"

She ran off in her golden high heels, and already had her finger on the bell when I called after her.

"Hey! Please don't tell him that you saw me here."

She waved to me and disappeared into the building.

I wasn't sure if she had understood me.

I also wasn't sure if I had understood her. Apparently Brenda knew more than I did. So Adam was still talking to her.

I felt betrayed, like a little kid who's not allowed to play with the other children.

What did the two of them have to discuss?

The neighboring table had barely been empty a second when a pair of scrappy gulls made for the remains of the meal and knocked over half a glass of beer. A young waitress came running and shooed the birds away.

I sat with Brenda at a restaurant in Malibu, two, three miles away from Cher's house, right on the ocean. When the wind was right, you could hear her playing tennis in her garden.

The waiter brought the check, and cleared my full plate. I hadn't touched a bite.

Brenda grabbed her brown leather credit card case and laid an American Express card down. Platinum. Then she slid her hand onto my forearm and stroked it as if it were that of a lover.

"Love, I'm so inexpressibly sorry."

I pulled my arm away, and the fat diamond ring on her hand hit the table with a dull click. Brenda reached for her cigarettes, and lit the last one in the pack.

"And you've really got to believe me. There's not another man.

Maybe you simply shouldn't have placed him under so much pressure."

I looked at my hands. My right thumb was running along the fingers of the other hand, tracing the course of the nail beds from the little finger to the thumb and back again. It seemed to me that I had never had so many wrinkles in my fingertips. Maybe I should move them less.

"In the end, it wouldn't have worked out anyway. Adam needs someone he can talk to. Who understands him one hundred percent. No offense meant, your English is awesome, but surely you wouldn't deny there's a certain language barrier."

My eyes wandered over to the Pacific. A couple of kids were playing in the water, and squealed happily as each new wave sloshed in. A brawny Saint Bernard jogged along the beach with his wispy owner. A young couple ran through the sand holding hands, stopping briefly so they could kiss. I wished for a really, really big wave.

"Ben? Are you coming?"

I felt her hand on my shoulder, and stood up. We walked to the parking lot in silence. There was still something she had to give me from Adam.

The first was this message:

"It would really mean a lot to Adam if the two of you could be friends."

So he knew that she had caught him in front of his building.

"Really be friends?" It reverberated in my head as if in an empty apartment once the cabinets have been removed and the paintings taken down.

His girlfriend with the wrinkly upper lip would apparently have the last word. I was speechless. Adam had done it with such ease.

On the way to our cars, I saw an old homeless woman in torn jeans; the left leg of her pants was several inches shorter than the other; her hair was long and matted.

43

She was asking people for money as they left the restaurant. Just now she was following a man in jeans and a leather jacket carrying a folder under his arm. Apparently he was in a hurry.

"Spare some change?" the woman asked in a friendly voice, holding her head at a slight angle.

"Sorry, I'm broke," a man in a suit protested, shrugged his shoulders, and drove off in his Porsche.

(In cities with streetcars like Berlin it's easier for the homeless: the riders can't get away if you start spare-changing between stops.)

I rummaged in my pockets for a couple of quarters, when Brenda opened her trunk and said something like: "Can you get it out? It's too heavy for me."

And now I was reunited with my yellow suitcase.

I locked the trunk and blinked into the impeccably blue sky. It was Friday noon; the sun was blazing, as it had been the last few days. I had done what I could to avoid it (the sun and self-pity don't really go well together): stayed in bed and killed a few bottles of red wine; sat in the movies; stumbled through empty museums or overfilled shopping malls, getting lost over and over again in branches of the Banana Republic, Abercrombie & Fitch, and Guess. And what chic names they always come up with for this cloney couture for bores; it's like hoping—in vain—to be surprised by the latest Meg Ryan movie.

Today I was happy to see the sun again, since in two and a half hours I would finally be on my flight back home. I was already running late, but it was a good day. Better than the previous ones, at any rate.

A night didn't pass without a call from Adam. I never spoke with him myself; more often than not, I had unplugged the phone in my room. There wasn't anything more to say. The notes and the faxes that the desk people gave me in the morning went directly into the wastebasket unread, as did his present, the sexy shorts.

It was over. Handing over the suitcase via Brenda was clear enough. Adam didn't want to know anything more about me.

"You probably wouldn't understand," he wrote in one of his faxes. Apparently he and Brenda agreed that I was too dull-witted to be spoken to.

"Surely you wouldn't deny there's a certain language barrier."

I hoped Adam would be happy with Brenda and her wrinkly lips. The Los Angeles experiment was over.

I made my new plans with the woman whose joy at my imminent return wasn't entirely unselfish.

"Who knows, something good'll come of it," Paula said, meaning Adam's betrayal. "Anyway, happy endings only exist in Hollywood."

We talked about moving in together, looking at apartments. She was even willing to give up her beloved Wilmersdorf if I would stop insisting on a cleaning lady twice a week.

In the morning I bought her some bath salts at Fred Segal (kind of like H&M with Prada prices), and collided with a chubby guy in sunglasses at the cash register, who on closer inspection turned out to be Alec Baldwin—my first celebrity of the year, but nonetheless a disappointing, second-class encounter considering that Fred Segal was the favorite store of stars like Brad Pitt and Jennifer Aniston.

As I was driving through Beverly Hills, past colossal film posters and house-high palm trees towering into the blue sky, I had something almost like a vacation feeling. I was even a little melancholy, and when I stopped at the light and saw a woman across the way jogging with her hair up and wearing a bright silk top, I thought, "Anyway, it's a shame, L.A., that nothing came of us. Don't take it personally."

All of a sudden I heard a crash. A second crash followed immediately after, and my car was shoved forward a few inches. Behind me a horn was sounding and wouldn't stop.

A crowd formed on the sidewalk; people came running out of nearby shops. Someone opened my door and asked if I was okay.

I got out and looked around. A black pickup truck hadn't braked, and crashed into the car behind me, which in turn was shoved into my back end.

My rear fender was hanging half off the car, the trunk lid was crumpled in the middle and was open a crack.

A pale little woman got out of the middle car, supported by an elderly man. At first glance she seemed uninjured, though she was holding her head with both hands.

When the doors of the pickup opened, two men appeared. The passenger was wearing tight blue jeans and a white shirt that was unbuttoned to his navel; stuck in his dyed black hair (in the sunlight you could detect the lighter roots) was a pair of sunglasses with big, dark lenses. As soon as he was on the street, he began talking excitedly to the driver, who had a striking face accentuated by his clean-shaven head, but then thrown off a bit by a thick mustache. He was dressed completely in black, and was fumbling around with his belt. A hint of stomach peeked out over his pants.

"It was my fault. I'm really sorry."

The mustache came up to me.

"Are you okay?"

He shook my hand and introduced himself as Scott.

"You don't have to worry about me," I said, and pointed to the woman from the car behind me. She was sitting on the sidewalk; someone had put a jacket across her shoulders.

"The police are on their way," someone yelled to me.

The friend of the mustache guy was standing next to us now and looked at me.

"Everything alright?" he asked, an octave higher than the mustache.

I looked at my watch.

"To be precise: I'm supposed to be on a plane in two hours. It'd be best if you could just give me your name and your insurance. I can't wait around for the police."

The guy in the white shirt took the sunglasses from his head and played with them. When he pushed up his sleeve, scratch marks were visible on his forearm. He noticed that I noticed.

"That was Roy, one of our cats, the dumb thing. Didn't want to be castrated."

I didn't say anything.

"I'm Pete. Where are you from?"

"Germany."

"I love Germany. Where from exactly?"

He ran his hand through his thin, dyed hair.

You might take the openness and friendliness of people in California as superficial, maybe even consider the locals dumb (there are even people there who think you drive on the left side of the road in Germany). But still the main thing is that they were friendly; that you wouldn't be hated here for wanting to order your food in a restaurant. And by the way, who in Germany knew that there were five Berlins in the USA? In Pennsylvania they even have their own East Berlin.

Still: I didn't find it a particularly apt moment for innocuous conversation, and raised my voice.

"Could we just get this settled now? Do you have something to write with?"

While Scott went over to the woman on the sidewalk, I followed his sidekick to the car. He dug around in the glove compartment for a pen.

"You on vacation here?

"Yeah, for a couple hours yet, like I said."

I looked over at the woman from the other car; she was rubbing her forehead. The mustache was talking to her, the sun reflecting off his cleanly shaved head.

The crowd around them was slowly dispersing.

"Shit! Scott? Do you have your driver's license handy?"

Pete stuck his sunglasses back into his thin hair and grinned at me. I'd really liked to have shoved his fucking sunglasses up his ass sideways, but I was afraid he might enjoy it.

"Tell me, how old are you?"

"Fifteen," I answered, annoyed.

Scott with his wide mustache trotted up slowly and held his documents out to his friend without a word. The friend indicated me with a nod of his head.

"He's so cute, huh?"

They grinned at me.

"Okay, can you two just cut it out?" It just burst out of me. "Maybe you two can go off somewhere later and jack each other off and be all nice and relaxed. All I want is your insurance information and whatever else I need, not your telephone number. I'm not interested in where you live and how many cats you have and which of them are castrated, okay?"

Two police cars turned the corner, and I ran with my papers to the cops so I could hit the freeway as soon as possible.

It certainly helped that Scott admitted right away it was his fault, but I still had to hang out for more than half an hour till everything had been sorted out.

As I was about to get into the car, Pete finally gave me a piece of paper with the requested information. He held his head somewhat at a tilt as he quoted a line from a Madonna song: "'The show is over, say goodbye.' I also wrote our address there. And the telephone number. In case there's anything wrong with the insurance. Y'understand?"

I didn't understand what there was to be understood, but I didn't have time to get all worked up about it. My flight was leaving in just one and a half hours. I was hot; I rolled my window down. Planes were climbing into the sky at short intervals, and I kept looking nervously at my watch to reassure myself that my flight wasn't one of those planes.

After ten minutes I hit the first traffic jam.

If I was still going to return the car rental, I could forget about my flight.

"Please let the flight be delayed! Just half an hour!"

I tried to nudge my way into the carpool lane, where only cars with at least three people are allowed. In Thailand, where there's a similar system, women earn money by standing at on-ramps to be picked up by businessmen who are in a hurry—in such a hurry that it wouldn't even occur to them to have sex with the women as well, as long as they're right there in the car. He who would like to be spared this expense sets up his inflatable sex doll in the passenger seat, much to the amusement of the police when they expose the scam.

It got better for about a mile. But that quickly came and went, and now all was at a standstill. Stopped in front of me was one of those black stretch limousines, inside which tourists always picture stars like Michael Jackson or Mariah Carey; but usually it's just other tourist groups (when you're splitting the fare ten ways, it's really not all that expensive) being chauffeured around the neighborhood in these decadent taxis.

I still had an hour and five minutes.

My head hurt. I cursed the police and Scott and Pete (y'understand?). The woman at Starbucks that morning who took ten minutes to do my latte (macchiato). I hated every single person who was in front of me on the freeway. I cursed Adam and his little girlfriend with the wrinkled upper lip. "I'm so happy to have Brenda at this difficult time" said one of the faxes he sent me at the hotel.

And then there was still a huge amount of hatred left over directed at me alone. For never being on time. For staying at a hotel in the middle of nowhere. For having to drive through Beverly Hills, of all places. For ever having met Adam. For breaking up with Poor Dull Daniel. And for having to stumble from one relationship to the next. I can't ever be alone.

"Happy endings only exist in Hollywood," Paula had said, and she was probably right.

When I finally reached my exit, I still had forty-three minutes. I tore down the street. Above me, one light after another was turning red, and my hands hurt because I was clenching the steering wheel so tensely to keep from spinning out at a curve.

At the airport, I ignored the sign for dropping off car rentals, headed directly for the international terminal and drove into the parking garage. Soaked with sweat, I dragged my suitcase out of the car, buckled on my rucksack and ran. On the way I threw all my luggage onto a trolley and tried to get past the other tourists as quickly as possible without injuring anyone.

My suitcase slipped off the luggage cart when I swerved around a kid who had crossed my path.

As I approached the check-in counter, cursing, an older couple turned around and regarded me with pity.

Even the woman behind the counter noted the commotion, and called to me over the other people in line:

"Where to, sir?"

I took an exhausted breath.

"Berlin."

CHAPTER 4

You have to learn not to let your happiness depend on other guys
anymore, irrespective of:
—the size of their ears
—their abundance of chest hair
—their talents in the kitchen and the bedroom

On the way to the kitchen I stumbled over empty wine bottles, their
clinking and jangling droning in my head. For a brief moment I was
tempted to count how many bottles we had knocked off yesterday,
but I quickly thought better of it.

"Anyone home?" I called out.

No answer.

Apparently I had the apartment to myself.

In the kitchen I found a full pot of fresh coffee—exactly how fresh
would soon become apparent—and a handwritten note.

"Do you have a horrible headache, too? Have fun!
    And stay as long as you want.
    Till tonight!"

I sat down on the patio with a cup of coffee and a glass of water, and
blinked into the sun. The harsh light stung my eyes, my head hurt,
probably from the accident still. Or maybe it'd make sense to count
the wine bottles after all?

It was early April, sometime in the morning.

A squirrel, a particularly fat one, peeked over the balustrade at the end of the patio, but took off rapidly when I wished him good morning.

I looked at my watch. It was a little before 1:00 p.m.

"Okay," I called after the squirrel, "I've slept through half the day, and I probably look like shit. No wonder, after what's happened the past few days!"

The plane to Berlin had taken off without me.

I raised a horrific cry in the terminal, howling and swearing at the other passengers, and above all at the woman behind the check-in counter because she wouldn't let me on the plane. Finally two security people accompanied me out of the building and hustled me and my luggage into a taxi.

I was so angry, I had the taxi take me to my rental, and raced back into the city as fast as I could. Sepulveda Boulevard, the longest street in Los Angeles, was blocked off for a film shoot, and from a distance you could see the big white trucks and countless people with headsets and walkie-talkies running around. So I had to jump over to the freeway, where the traffic jam had in the meantime divided itself equally in both directions.

My heart was just about flipping over when an hour later I stood at Adam's door, ringing the bell furiously. I thought I saw him at the window, but wasn't sure. Nothing happened. I cursed the day. I thought if I had to wait a minute more, I would burst. If there had been a blood pressure meter on my arm, it would have exploded.

I ran to my car and kicked the right side, whereby the damaged fender fell clanking to the street.

What had Pete said?

"I also wrote our address there. And the telephone number. In case there're any problems. Y'understand?"

I remembered seeing something about Bel Air on the piece of paper, and jumped back into the car.

They would have to put me up somewhere—I didn't care how, I didn't care where—until I could finally fly back to Germany. They owed me that. I had no intention of going back to that stinking hotel.

When I turned into the street for their apartment, they were just carrying grocery bags into the building.

I made an enormous scene, explained about Adam and the missed flight, and how they had fucked up not just my day but my entire life.

"You owe me one shitty favor, and by the way: Your earlier come-ons were the last, and you should by no means think that I've come here to jump into bed with one of you! I'd probably catch something unimaginable."

For a brief moment they looked at me as if they wanted to clobber me. But instead they apologized and brought my things into the building.

Their apartment was very big and bright; one entire wall of the huge living room consisted of windows. Up in the mountains you could see the famous Getty Museum glowing, this grey-beige beauty, for which a white façade had originally been planned but the residents of Bel Air had successfully prevented it because they didn't want to be constantly blinded by it.

They had a parquet floor, not typically American. On a gigantic sofa—color: bottle-green—with long fringe hanging from the backrest lay gold pillows bordered with strings. In front of it stood a rectangular glass table with rounded edges. The plate of glass was resting on a white ceramic base that reminded you of a mixture between a wave and a kneeling man. Whatever these guys did for a living, they certainly weren't interior decorators. Or at best: unemployed interior decorators.

Pete showed me to the guestroom, which was both fringe- and string-free. The bed smelled freshly made; there were flowers on the nightstand. A lazy tomcat—who was introduced to me as Roy, the Freshly Castrated—lay on the windowsill.

I began to feel embarrassed and wanted to get out of there, when Scott appeared in the door and said I had to at least stay until Sunday. They were expecting a couple of friends over for a barbecue, and wouldn't think of letting me leave before.

Pete made a face I wouldn't soon forget.

Okay, let's back up. The whole thing from the beginning.

Hello, I'm Ben. Hey, nice shoes! Would you like to get a drink with me? No, really, you're a Leo, too? What a coincidence! Wanna come home with me? Which side of the bed do you sleep on? How do you take your coffee? How come we only listen to your CDs in the car? Do you really plan on wearing that shirt to the party when everyone can see your nipples through it? Please, let's just stay home; they're *your* friends. Could you maybe just once clean up the sink after you shave? Sorry, I'm just not in the mood. Sorry, I don't know what's up with me either. No, it has nothing to do with you. No, I haven't met anyone. What's on TV right now?

Everything again from the beginning, like in school when I had to repeat a grade when my parents died. The same dumb questions all over again, for which I still didn't have the correct answers. New dumb tests, new unnecessary misunderstandings, until you finally moved on to a new level and had to deal with a whole new set of problems. A new level like in those computer games where first you have to get past all these hairy monsters unharmed, even though they're trying to eat you, in order to reach the next level, an endless labyrinth teeming with trapdoors as well as with new, bigger, not-quite-as-hairy monsters. And when you've survived even that, suddenly you're being shot at from all sides and you can either duck the bullets or jump over them, and once you have this level under your belt, at some point it just gets boring and you turn the thing off.

Game over.

Welcome to Level One. You have no points. Choose a degree of difficulty. As if once you turned thirty you didn't have it tough enough. Just going out was torture. What should you wear? Is it time for muted colors, the beige cardigan, the matt gray vest? Or can you still wear the corduroy with the wide cuffs a couple more years without losing face? A great deal of concentration must also go into the appropriate holding of one's head. You hold it too high, it looks arrogant; too low, and one of your double chins is visible.

After three beers you start thinking about switching over to water. Not at all because you're so terribly reasonable and remember that you're driving, but because you can't handle it as well as you used to, and after the last party couldn't see right for two days.

Anyway: With the local beers that they serve you in America, you can drink four or five without experiencing a noticeable change of consciousness. Another good thing: You always get to bed early. Other than a few after-hours parties on the weekend, the bars and clubs in L.A. close every night at 2:00—a time at which Berliners are just checking their track-suit jackets at the coatroom. But Californians like Adam are really athletic in the morning, and that doesn't work when you're just getting to bed as the sun comes up.

I took his photo from my wallet, the one of him that I shot at Joshua Tree. He was leaning on one of the huge boulders and refreshing himself by pouring the last drops from a water bottle over his chest.

Slowly I traced my finger over his wet chest hair, and then took the photo in both hands to tear it up. But then I decided not to, and stuck it back in my wallet, all the way in the back where it would soon be forgotten.

"And how did you really get to know the two of them?"

A pair of big, blue-gray eyes looked me over; the left eyebrow was arched and grandly raised. The man to whom this agile eyebrow belonged was leaning back in his chair, gnawing on a stalk of celery.

Scott protested loudly as Pete got up to go get some more ice water. He was wearing a T-shirt with "Material Girl" in glitter lettering.

"Well, I find the story totally believable," threw in a cheeky little Latino who was sitting next to the eyebrow artist, whom he then pinched on the left nipple. It was pierced. You could tell through his shirt.

Siegfried, the other cat, also castrated, was lying on his lap letting itself be petted.

"One morning Scott found his driver's license in his cornflakes, did he ever tell you that?"

"I think he must've had sex with that woman who gave him the driver's test. Huh, darling?" Gavin, the eyebrow artist, dunked the remainder of his celery stalk into a bowl of sharp curry sauce. "You just drove one short time around the block, during which you ran a stop sign and hit two old people and a cat. So when the test lady went to get out of the car, you took care of her. In reverse, as it were."

"I don't think that's something any of you boys have quite managed," a pretty, young Chinese woman in a Lakers cap called out from the end of the table.

Pete placed a pitcher of water on the table in front of her and laid his left hand on her shoulder; the right one he ran through his thinning hair as he looked at me.

"Was it really difficult for you to get used to driving on the right side of the road?"

"Darling, you're a little confused there," Scott jumped in. He looked at his boyfriend as if he wanted to stick him in a home. At the same time, he seemed happy to be able to change the subject.

"Driving on the left is in England and South Africa. Everybody knows that."

Pete pushed his lower lip slightly over the upper, and sat down again.

"Well noted, Scott," I said to defuse the situation.

"We're the ones who speed like crazy on the autobahn. But then, we're also the ones who actually ease up on the gas when they come to a red light."

Gavin and his Latino friend bellowed with laughter.

Scott grimaced.

"Don't you have to be getting home soon, young man?"

"No, the gentlemen of the house have kindly placed a room at my disposal after having attempted to kill me this afternoon," I said, and grinned at him. He raised his beer to me as a toast.

Somehow I liked him; I even felt a kind of sympathy for Pete. Or was it pity? He was at the level of your average *People Magazine* reader, maybe crossed with an *Entertainment Weekly* subscriber, and he considered the line "All the world's a stage, and all the men and women merely players" to have originated with Madonna.

You had to give him credit, though: He could identify any one of her songs after just three seconds, without confusing "Who's That Girl?" with "La Isla Bonita"—and Madonna herself probably can't even do that.

Besides, he had a rough childhood behind him. Once a week his mother left the house with an old toothbrush, and spent the entire afternoon scrubbing Joanne Woodward's star on the Walk of Fame.

"Is that your latest scam for abducting defenseless young boys? How old are you anyway, Ben?"

Gavin's Latino friend emptied his glass and let Scott fill it again.

"Thirty-one, and not the least bit defenseless."

"I didn't want to know how old you'll be in a few years! How old are you really?"

His little jokes were getting annoying, and I turned to my neighbor at the table. Up until now he had laughed along with us but had otherwise been dull and reserved, and after two bites of salad had ceased food intake. A full glass of wine, untouched, stood before him. The surface of the wine rippled like a lake stirred by a soft breeze.

I leaned back in my chair. Under the table I could see how he was fidgeting with his right foot, which he had placed over the left.

"And you? How do you know these two?" I asked him.

For the first time I noticed his small, green eyes. They seemed a bit dreamy, but maybe he was also just tired.

"We work out together," said James.

"He calls that working out!" Scott called from across the table. "James tortures us three times a week. I think he hates us. We invite him to dinner hoping next time he'll be nicer to us."

I looked at him. James had short, dark hair, no sideburns and full lips, the lower of which was somewhat sexier.

"And? Are you?"

"No, I can't be bribed."

This wasn't exactly the world's wittiest comeback, something to throw you off your chair and have you pounding the floor, but then again he had these sexy eyes. And anyway: I could be the witty one.

"Good boy," I said, unwavering.

Pete started telling us about two guys he'd seen in the shower at the gym. One of them had spoken to Scott and …

"What're you up to here in L.A.?" James asked. His fidgety foot was making me nervous. I explained that my plans had disintegrated, and that I was soon flying back to Germany. At first I didn't want to mention Adam, but then I told him the whole story.

"Do you not like it in California anymore?"

He was also really big and buff, once you took a longer look at him. But it didn't make him look like a blown-up balloon. All in all, very well put together.

"Not at all. I had thought about moving here before I even met Adam. Actually, every fall and always in winter."

"And now you're flying back?" he asked.

Apparently James considered this a silly idea.

"First you go there because of Adam, and now you want to leave again because of Adam!" Paula had said. "What is it you want, actually?"

Maybe they were both right.

I looked at him and began to nod slowly. In the silence I thought I heard a rustling caused by the nervous tapping of his foot. The nodding of my head seemed in some absurd way to be in sync with the tapping of his foot, and I stopped it.

I told him about the Hollywood newspaper column, but quickly added that of course I would also be writing articles as a political observer, as the case may be. I didn't want him thinking he was dealing with some chintzy little gossip reporter.

The Latino leaned over to me and laid his hand on my shoulder.

"Who are the three most interesting people you've ever interviewed?"

This guy was like a walking questionnaire.

"No idea. It's very seldom, really, that I do interviews."

"Okay, if I could wish for who I'd wanna meet ..."

He turned back to the whole group around the table so he could really wow them with his utterly original answer. His hand was still on my shoulder.

"... then: Hillary Clinton. And then the Pope. And Nicole Kidman. And I'd ask her if she and Tom Cruise had ever ..."

I looked to James and mouthed a silent "Help!" But he grinned, stood up, excused himself and went to the bathroom.

I hated him. But not for long, because all of a sudden Gavin sat down at the empty place next to me.

"I heard you're looking for a job," he whispered in a conspiratorial tone.

"Yeah."

"What do you feel like doing?"

"It sounds as if you know about something," I said, and watched with awe as he once again executed his eyebrow trick.

"Our theater—I'm an actor—our theater can always use help. Actually there's a bunch of jobs: a little press work; putting together the monthly schedule; selling tickets sometimes. It's just a small theater, and we're closed Monday through Wednesday. Maybe you can stop by sometime."

It was on Sunset Boulevard in West Hollywood. According to Gavin's description, it was the place where Adam and I had seen the Callas thing. I wasn't sure whether it would be a good idea to work there.

Just then the general conversation swept over us. People were fantasizing about the alleged lover of the Mission Impossible Tom Cruise and his alleged and unspeakable sex video. There followed a discussion as to whether it was really easier for scientologists to overcome reading disabilities (Tom Cruise had claimed something to that effect), and why they always wanted to get their pilot's license (Pete claimed this, and named as examples the Mission Impossible Tom Cruise and the far more impossible John Travolta).

It was the unanimous opinion of the group, by the way, that Tom Cruise was a dreamboat, upon which I remarked that I could well do without men who were only a head taller than a parking meter.

At that moment, a roughly two-parking-meter man returned from the bathroom and resumed his old seat, which Gavin gave up with good grace and no questions asked, as if James and I had been married for ten years.

I ignored him, and asked Scott if there was still any wine to be had.

"Now he's probably thinking that I'm thinking he's hotter than a dozen sailors for me," James probably thought and looked at me curiously.

"Now he's probably thinking that I'm hot as ten sailors for him," I thought, and noted that in reality it was at least fifteen.

A lot of gay guys—the cheap ones, at least—would have tried to drag the good James into bed as quickly as possible to grab onto that great dark hair of his and to lick his muscular arms. They would have been wowed by those sexy green eyes.

They would have laid siege that very evening, asked for his number or given him theirs.

How cheap!

"Sco-ottttt!" I yelled after all the guests had departed. "When are you going to the gym again for a workout?"

"I knew you'd like him."

He was just emptying the dishwasher.

"Tell me!" I badgered.

"I'm shocked. You Germans are really awful. What's become of Adam so quickly?

"Adam who?" I said, and nibbled a bit of the last remaining brownie.

"Okay, if it's that important: the day after tomorrow," he said.

"What's wrong with tomorrow?"

Pete brought bowls back in from the living room.

"James thought you were nice, honey. Said so as he left. But I wasn't supposed to tell you."

I looked over at Scott, triumphant.

"The guy's got taste," I said.

"James isn't for you, believe me."

Scott put the last plate into the dishwasher and closed the door.

"My god, he bores me to death every time I see him!" Pete said.

I looked at the two of them.

"I'm not looking to marry him. Just wanna get my hands on him, that's all. Good night, you two."

Before I fell asleep, I suddenly thought of a story that Yifei, the Chinese woman, had told me.

She has moved to Los Angeles shortly before she married Keith, an American professional basketball player, but she still didn't have her permanent green card. And just getting married wasn't enough to get it.

The immigration officials conducted one of their notorious interviews to find out how genuine the marriage was. It came off as a mixture between a cross-examination and one of those unbelievable how-well-do-you-know-each-other games with which relatives and friends try to compromise the bridal pair at wedding receptions (which is even worse than a cross-examination).

The official asked them questions alternately.

Where does your wife work? What's the name of your husband's company?

Where was Yifei born? What's his mother's first name?

What did she think of her husband? What did Keith like about her?

"Do you like your mother-in-law?"

"Yes, she gave me this watch."

"Can I call her right now to confirm that?"

"Be my guest."

But that still wasn't enough. They wanted to see pictures that showed the two of them together. Pictures from their wedding and vacations. Yifei and Keith had to submit letters, printouts of e-mails they had written to each other. The official skimmed through a few random passages.

The two spent more than an hour in his office until he had finally been convinced that they weren't strangers who had gotten married for a green card. Supposedly the interrogation had lasted so long, according to Yifei, because to outside observers their size difference (nearly two feet) made them come off as an unlikely couple.

I petted Siegfried's neck, who had jumped right up onto my stomach doing a really good imitation of the whirring of an electric train I had played with as a kid.

I sighed blissfully and wondered what the name of the gym was where James worked.

CHAPTER 5:

You shouldn't have sex with men over 45 unless:
—they look like they're 25
—they can plausibly assure you that they're 35, or
—it's been 45 years since you had sex

Adam's white pickup truck is standing beneath the streetlight. Even at a distance I can see the thing glowing.

Before I can decide where I'll apply the key, I walk around it two times slowly.

I decide on the driver's door, the window of which is sporting a large dried dollop of bird shit. I set the key next to the lock and scrape it across the door all along the side to the rear. The screech is deafening, like in school when the teacher would hit the wrong angle with the chalk on the blackboard. I scrape a second line into the white finish parallel to the first. And then a third. Somewhere above me an owl hoots in a tree; the wind pushes an empty McDonald's bag down the street.

I take a step back and appraise my work.

Pleased, I shift over to the other side of the pickup and scratch up the other door. Maybe it's just my imagination, but the passenger side seems to make three times as much noise, as if it were trying to alert the neighbors or the police. I'm happy with just two long scratch marks on this side.

At one of the nearby houses, someone slams a window shut with a loud scrunch. Am I being watched?

I nonchalantly pull a knife from my pants pocket and go into a crouch.

The front right tire makes a loud pfffffffft as I jab the blade into the rubber. It's also very difficult to pull it out again, but I do. After doing the same to the left front tire, I sit on the sidewalk and watch as the pickup goes to its knees, like a big polar bear. Very slowly.

I can already hear the police sirens in the distance, but I'm not quite finished yet.

I open the tailgate on the pickup and pull out a big sledge hammer. It nearly falls on my foot, it's so heavy.

The first police car turns into the street; two others follow.

Suddenly the street is ablaze with lights.

With all my might I drag the tool to the front of the car. I aim for the windshield and let 'er rip.

A big, good-looking man in uniform jumps out of the first car and fires a shot. There's a bang; the bullet has hit one of the pickup's rear tires.

The hammer falls to the street with a thud. I slowly turn around.

James drops his weapon and smiles at me. We run to each other, then he wraps me in his arms and carries me to his car.

Tires squealing, we speed out of there.

My mother, who's sitting next to my father in the backseat, urges us not to drive so fast, she's already quite queasy.

My father hands her a barf bag and asks whether anyone would like coffee or tea.

I'm the first to spot Paula. She's strolling along the median strip; in her right hand she's holding a parasol.

"Stop!" I yell at James. But he yells back that he can't brake, and shifts into a higher gear.

Paula is just ten yards away; she hasn't noticed us yet.

Behind us a whole squadron of police cars is getting closer, with sirens and red-white-and-blue lights.

Paula's parasol flies up into the air. It buckles once as we drive over it.

I woke up soaked with sweat and out of breath, but greatly relieved.

I got along very well with 50% of my hosts—with Scott, even if his know-it-all attitude was a bit much to bear sometimes. He reminded me of Poor Dull Daniel; both were the same age, early forties. I also found it annoying when he would kiss me on the lips every day to say good morning. What disturbed me about it wasn't so much his big mustache as the fact that it was an open-mouth kiss, and every time he did it I was afraid he was suddenly going to start madly tonguing me, which I wasn't sure I wanted.

The other half was rarely home, and was just as rarely missed by either me or Scott, it seemed. Pete worked as a flight attendant, and vanished for a few days right after the barbecue.

"Good luck looking for a room!" This was his farewell line, even though I hadn't announced any such intention. I wasn't sure who Pete trusted less, me or his boyfriend. But obviously he hoped I would have vanished from the communal apartment by the time he returned from god-knows-where.

The poor guy was jealous.

"Give yourself time. You don't have to take the first room that comes along," Scott said, and kissed me with a slightly open mouth.

So I took the first job that came along as the ticket-selling press rep on Sunset Boulevard (I had my first good luck in a while: Gavin really went to bat for me). It actually was the theater Adam and I had gone to, but Callas, or rather the poor parody of her, had left the theater a few weeks ago and moved to New York, along with the guy, just incidentally, whose job as press-repping ticket seller I now had.

It was a perfect supplement to my work for the newspaper (not necessarily in financial terms, though I couldn't live on the proceeds from the stuff I sold back in Germany for long—not counting the capital gain from my favorite books). Midday I'd sit in the park and write my column, and then I'd go to the theater for four or five hours and take ticket orders on the phone; I also tried to write copy about upcoming shows that would give the press and the public the feeling that we were dealing with hit shows here (not always easy at a theater that casts female roles like Callas with flamers). In between I still had enough time to research stories for my column.

The first installment met with modest success. My favorite part of it went:

> "Our town is about to become nicer! Everyone can rejoice as the worst actress in the universe, Demi Moore, has announced that she doesn't want to come back to Hollywood.
>
> But new disasters are in the wings: At the top of the American movie hit parade since last weekend is a Formula One movie with Sylvester Stallone. You think that's bad news? There's more appalling to come, because the supporting cast includes such German nonentities as Till Schweiger, Verona Feldbusch and Blümchen.
>
> It's a shame that they couldn't get Susan Stahnke, perhaps as the representative for a line of handy urinals for race car drivers on the go."

In the edited version that Carstensen e-mailed back to me every other sentence was crossed out with the comment: "I like this a lot; unfortunately it's unprintable. Don't you have sex there in America? Relax already! C"

Things weren't going all that well in the sex/relaxation area either.

James turned out to be an arrogant asshole (which didn't make him entirely unattractive). The first time I went to his gym with Scott, he acted as if we'd never seen each other before. No conversation, not even small talk. Not exactly a compliment to my quick, uncomplicated decision to stay, for a start, in Los Angeles. (Hadn't he suggested it himself the night of the barbecue?) No sincerely admiring "Great how you've put the split with Adam behind you!", also no overdue invitation to dinner. A brief "Hi, howaya?" before he ran me through every fucking machine in the place, an even shorter "Seeya!", and that was it.

"You have to give him time," Paula said.

"He's had five days."

"Don't you think you could give yourself a little break? Ten days ago you still wanted to live with Adam. By the way, he wrote to you."

I screamed in pain when I tried to pull my knees up as I lay on the sofa. Every cell in my body hurt. Even breathing was torture, depending on my position, and scratching my ear or the back of my neck was simply out of the question.

It was a great relief when I'd rub my head along the back of the sofa. I picked that up from one of the castrated toms.

"Unfortunately Adam didn't want to live with me anymore, if you remember. That made the matter somewhat difficult. And you can burn that letter. I don't want to read it."

I was really terrific at not understanding what Paula wanted to say to me.

"By the way, lately I've been destroying his car at night."

"What?"

"In my dreams. Scratch the finish; puncture the tires; the whole deal. And then James comes along …"

"Let me guess: on a white stallion."

"No, in a black-and-white police car. And you don't need to say 'white stallion.' That's like 'Adam the Asshole' or 'The Fabulous James.' 'Stallion' says it all on its own."

There was a rerun of a *Golden Girls* episode on the TV, one of the later ones, when it wasn't funny anymore.

I tried to reach for the remote that was lying right in front of me on the table, but apparently my arm had shrunk a few inches from the workout.

"Okay, you've been without a man for ten days now. Do you think you can make it another ten?"

"What for?"

"So maybe you can find out how nice it can be to be alone for a while, Ben."

Like you? I thought, but refrained from saying it out loud. The last man Paula slept with was Konrad's father the day Konrad was conceived. This was probably one of the reasons why I was always so welcome at her house.

"I can be alone when I'm fifty and have to pay for sex. That'll be really nice."

"I didn't say you should give up sex— Hang on a second …"

I heard her talking in the background to Konrad. He sounded excited.

"Sorry, I'll have to go soon. Where were we?"

"Is there a problem?"

"With Konrad? I don't know. He got beat up at school yesterday, but he didn't tell me why. And now his shoulder hurts."

I hoped that Paula hadn't sent him to school in a hand-crocheted cap.

"If somebody doesn't like the way he dresses, they should just leave him alone," she used to say. Real life seemed to indicate that the exact opposite was true, but Paula had little luck with this theory.

"Is it bad?" I asked.

"I'm not sure. Nobody saw anything."

"I was never quite sure back in the day why those guys had it in for me. And when it stopped, you know what? I didn't understand that either."

Anyway, I knew one thing: If I were given the choice between ever setting foot inside a gym again and being beaten up, I wouldn't have to deliberate for long.

"They were probably all afraid of your big girlfriend Paula," said my big girlfriend Paula.

"It'd nice if you were here. Say hello to Konrad for me."

"I will," she said.

"And tell him to let these idiots know: If they don't leave him alone, he's gonna sic his gay uncle from America on them, who's got a couple extra pair of handcuffs he currently doesn't need."

"They'll quake with fear. Have you found a room yet? If you're still there in July, I'm coming for a visit. Konrad will be on vacation then, and I can do without the Love Parade."

Actually I had found a few rooms; I just didn't want to move into any of them. One was too small, another was dilapidated and filthy, yet another was too dark, the next too expensive. ("You're pretty picky, honey!" Pete had said, who was still jealous. "This is L.A., y'know?")

In one apartment you could barely stand the stink because the half-dead proprietress owned a parakeet, two turtles, and a dog, which I could walk once a day to reduce my rent.

I nearly fainted in the next one because there were cigarette butts smoldering in every room. So I found myself incapable of following for very long the commentary of the landlord, a Japanese guy with a ponytail of white hair. He had set up the apartment according to feng shui, and at every window stood vases, candles, and odd little wood carvings—each assigned the task of neutralizing negative external influences.

"Do you know why I initially decided to move in here?"

I still remember.

"The entrance to the building faces east, the direction of the sunrise. That means wealth. And success."

Presumably you had to believe in it for it to work. At any rate, I wasn't ready to increase his wealth as a boarder.

I had a good feeling the day after when a likeable guy opened the door. Colin had apparently just gotten up, since he was only wearing a bathrobe. I took him to be mid-forties; he had slightly graying temples and a sportily trimmed beard with one gray spot on the right just above his chin.

His apartment was impressively neat, no newspapers or shoes were lying around, and the remote was sitting on the right edge of the table. Classical music played softly from invisible speakers. The apartment was sparsely furnished but tasteful. No plants.

He offered me a chair in his kitchen, from which there was a terrific view of the mountains, and poured me a glass of wine.

"Make yourself comfortable. I hope you're okay here. Excuse me a moment."

He left me alone.

I took a big, thirsty swig of the wine, and in my mind saw Paula and James dancing through the kitchen.

"Terrific party!" they called to me. "How did you land this place?"

"Confess, you must have had sex with him."

As I rose from my seat to offer a toast, Colin's calling me pulled me out of my reverie.

I set my wineglass down and went to look for him.

He lay naked on his bed, his feet bound with the belt from the bathrobe, and looked at me expectantly.

CHAPTER 6

You shouldn't have sex with guys who afterwards immediately
stick a cigarette in their mouth unless:
—the only alternative is to have sex with guys who stick a cigarette in their mouth right before
—it's a way of keeping them from blathering on about idiotic
   things or asking you what you were just thinking about, or
—the sex with them is so good that you want to have a cigarette
   right afterwards

It was shortly before sunset, and I was afraid of remaining deaf for
the rest of my life.

After working at the theater, I went to see a little pierced woman
with green hair who deejayed at the big clubs in L.A. and was just
listening to some new CDs as I got to the apartment. It took at least a
quarter of an hour before she finally heard me knocking at the door,
which at first I tried to coordinate by knocking in between the rapid
house-music beats, and then, just for variety, pounded steadily for
two minutes straight.

She was listening to these CDs really, really loud, so loud that at
first I wasn't sure whether she was saying she'd prefer to rent the
room to a female or if she wanted to sell me drugs. Probably I just
hadn't understood the rental price correctly.

"Who exactly are you trying to prove something to?" I asked myself as I got back into the car afterwards, exhausted. To be precise, it
was Paula's question after I had shared with her the first few install-

ments of my search for a room, and she sounded as if she already had an answer, but she didn't want to reveal it to me.

I'd just stopped at a light in West Hollywood—the car in front of me was sporting one of those ridiculous "My Son Is a Student of the Month at Gag Me with a Spoon University" stickers—when I saw in the dark blue Thunderbird on my left a totally sweet thing with curly black hair, who in turn had just discovered a totally sweet thing with funny ears in the car on his right.

As we took off from the light, we smiled at each other.

After a couple of miles, I passed him and we smiled a bit again. I saw in the side mirror that he was staying just a bit behind me and was trying to match my speed. A black stretch limo was creeping along in front of me, so I switched lanes; as I drove past, some young Asian women rolled down her window, waving and yelling something to me I couldn't make out.

The Thunderbird popped up again in my rearview mirror. I suddenly had a vision entailing various bodily fluids. It plays out in the passenger seat of a vintage American car, the windows are fogged up and no one can see in or out. If the insanely fat woman just disappearing into the 7 Eleven around the corner were more observant, she'd notice the wondrous rocking of the car and the fact that in the past five minutes its position had shifted a couple of inches by the time she was back on the street with a candy bar.

His honk ended the wondrous rocking as he slowly drove past me. Again we smiled at each other. What can I say? To an outside observer the whole procedure was as conspicuous as it was silly and, above all, as drawn-out.

For this reason, at this point I'd like to direct the reader's attention to the points of interest on either side of Santa Monica Boulevard: If you're driving toward the beach (incidentally the home stretch for Route 66), on the right side on a small hill is the imposing Los Angeles Temple, a grand structure finished in 1956, at that time the largest temple of the Church of Latter Day Saints and whose façade consists of a mixture of crushed quartz and white Portland cement. The land on which the temple and its well-tended garden are situated originally belonged to the 20s silent screen star and pioneer stuntman Harold Lloyd, who was awarded an honorary Oscar over fifty years ago for being a master comedian. The church acquired the sizeable chunk of land from Lloyd for $175,000.

On the left side of the road, at the foot of a big movie billboard, you can see the remnants of tracks that had been filled up and cemented over back in the 70s. This was thanks to the large auto companies that moved to Los Angeles at the time with the intention of freeing the locals of the fourth-worst scourge of their existence (after body hair, nicotine, and aging): the streetcar. They were successful, and in the end it seemed a fair deal: one car for each and every person in lieu of a streetcar for everyone. Unfortunately, they didn't teach the Los Angelinos how to drive on wet, rainy streets, about which they're usually extremely wary, like Berliners are about ice storms, which don't occur as frequently. When it rains in Los Angeles, everyone comes late to work.

Then, stretching to the Pacific were a McDonald's next to a Carl's Jr. next to a Burger King next to a Taco Bell next to a Subway's next to an In-N-Out Burger, and in between sat a German car repair shop. That's where I gave Curls Man a sign and turned on my right blinker.

He had these plump cheeks, which is where some guys store whatever baby fat they haven't lost.

"Hey!" he called as he got out of his car and lit a cigarette. The guy had no ass at all, but I didn't really care—I had an ass of my own.

"Hey," I said as the door shut behind me.

"Why don't we go somewhere? I live just a couple blocks away."

I liked his eloquent reserve, and followed him to his apartment.

"Everything's bigger here," a cabdriver told me the first time I came to the USA as an exchange student. And for years I never had any reason to doubt it.

The fat little squirrel that skittered around the patio some mornings at Scott and Pete's was certainly living proof that "bigger" by no means also meant "prettier."

And then along came Thunderbird with his plump cheeks.

I have never—and at the end of this book I'll provided the names of a few witnesses along with photos and telephone numbers—never demanded a lot of guys. It's repellent to me when people rate their sexual partners purely according to their physical endowments and then correspondingly lust after them or reject them.

But I allow myself one qualification, and you can call it superficial, I can live with that: I'm fine with celebrating the smaller things in life—provided you can find them. Or, to be fair: It shouldn't disappear entirely when you take it in your hand.

On the other hand, I often wonder when I'm reading personal ads or hanging out in a sex chat room, how do guys actually live with these horrible 9" disabilities. Do they have to wear special underwear? Does their health insurance cover the cost of having to buy extra-large condoms? And what formula do they use to calculate their body mass index?

But as I said: Thunderbird Man came, he smoked a quick one, and I left. In the car I decided that not only was nearly everything in America bigger, but it was also more convenient. I had never been so grateful to drive an automatic.

There's this website where you can register for free and that will, based on various specifications, find you the perfect roommate or at least suggest several perfect roommates. A system that—applied to personal ads or as a checklist before going out on a first date—could prevent guys from making dumb mistakes and could even make them happy. Among these specifications are: Use of Alcohol and Drugs (Never? Seldom? Sometimes? Often?); Personal Hygiene (you had five degrees—from "clean" to "a real mess"—to choose from); and Sleeping Habits (Does it have to be totally quiet? Are little noises okay? Semi-loud noises? An outright din?)

How many nights have I lain next to men who couldn't fall asleep without the TV on? Or some Barbra Streisand CD that had a skip on the fourth track. Whereby I had a legitimate reason to get up and turn off the music while my host was enjoying a deep and sound sleep. Unfortunately right on my arm. And when I had finally freed my arm and found the right button on the stereo system, the blissful sleeper began to snore because he'd flipped onto his back, and I'd really have much preferred hearing "Somewhere over the Rainbowbowbowbow …" again.

None of the things I found on the website particularly interested me—since who wants to live in industrial Burbank or boring old Calabasas when they get the same room in West Hollywood for twice the money?

I was about to log off when a new ad appeared on the screen that noticeably improved my mood.

Good location: Beverly Hills; acceptable price: $550 (of course, in Berlin for that kind of money you could get an apartment with several rooms and two balconies; though, to be honest, it's not like you can sit on both of them at the same time!). Victor, as the author of this ad was called, had a compatible Cleanliness Level (average), and as far as alcohol consumption went, our self-assessments coincided perfectly: occasional. It only remained to be seen whether Victor had also lied about this.

I sent him an e-mail with Scott's telephone number.

The ink on the "Send" confirmation wasn't even dry when the phone rang. It was James.

"Hey, you still remember me? We met a few days ago at Pete and Scott's, at dinner."

Of course I remembered quite precisely. And I remembered even better the night at the gym when he treated me like a rusty barbell.

"Hang on a sec … uhhh: James, James … We sat next to each other, right."

"So you've decided to stay here," he said.

Strictly speaking, I had only decided not to go back right away. It depended on a number of factors. James just should have been nicer.

"We'll see. That's what Victor thinks, too," I said.

A short pause.

"Victor's your ex, right."

"No, that was Adam," I said.

"Okay. So Victor is …?"

"Mid-thirties, clean, and I might be moving in with him."

"That was quick."

James sounded disappointed.

"Yeah, I just e-mailed him about it. He could be calling right away. Can I give Scott or Pete a message?"

"What? No, thanks a lot," he said.

Score: 1:1.

The next day I took off first thing in the morning for Beverly Hills. I felt good, even though I'd had a bad night. Bitterly, oh how bitterly, did I regret my victory over James!

What if I didn't have any more chances with him?

What if he considered me some horrible little floozie who—when he isn't being dumped by his boyfriend or stumbling into questionable adventures on Santa Monica Boulevard—is indiscriminately dragging men into his apartment.

In front of the building was a small, well-tended garden in which there was a row of birds-of-paradise, whose blooms reminded me of gaudily made-up drag queens.

I promised myself I could call James later as a reward if my visit with Victor was successful, and rang the bell.

A well-groomed guy in a light gray suit, barefoot, opened the door. He held a cup of tea in his hand.

"Hi, Victor. I'm here about the ad."

"My name's Robert, but please come in."

A dog yapped at me, some type of poodle that looked like a sheep with long, thin legs and an equally thin snout. The aversion was mutual; the hysterical barking just wouldn't stop.

"It's great you could come so quickly. Actually, you were the first one to respond to the ad. I want to rent the room as soon as possible."

"And Victor …"

"I'll just show it to you real quick. I have to be at work in a few minutes."

He took a big swig from his cup.

The room was about 150 square feet and was fully furnished. That is, there was a big (long enough for James), wide bed (I could very easily fit in next to him, and you can always get used to sleeping on your side—but why should I sleep anyway? Isn't that impolite when you have a visitor?), a table, and a wardrobe; the room also had its own telephone connection. It smelled of paint; apparently it had just been renovated. The window looked out on a small backyard.

That was my room

"This is my room," I informed Robert, overjoyed.

"Cool."

"And Victor lives here, too?

I followed Robert into his bedroom, where he pulled on a pair of dark blue socks.

"Yeah. Is that a problem for you?"

"That depends."

"Sorry, that's what it said in the ad."

He stood up and pulled a shoe out from under the bed.

I wasn't sure whether I had read the ad carefully enough.

"I'd just like to talk with him before I decide."

"Whatever you want. I don't know that it'll help all that much, but … VICTOR!"

The ugly dog came scampering around the corner and licked its master's hand. Its fur was like the stuff of my early childhood nightmares: a cap with built-in earflaps that made me the laughingstock of the school on a seasonal basis. I've hated the period between November and March ever since.

Robert stood up with a shoe in his hand, walked past me and stopped at the door. He looked at me seriously.

"Good luck. Sometimes you can't get a word in edgewise with this one."

CHAPTER 7

You shouldn't move in with guys who write poems about butterflies and spring meadows, unless:
—you don't have to read them
—you don't have to say they're good
—you have no other choice

Robert wanted to show the room to one other person, and after that
he'd make a decision.

Just to be safe, I looked at still another apartment in Los Feliz,
sort of a Prenzlauer-Bergish area that, like its Berlin counterpart,
had been taken over by artists. Whoever considered himself to be
one, lived there. Maybe I was about to meet a sweet young actor
who threw regular parties with his famous colleagues, and I'd rent
a room from him. In my mind I'm already celebrating the house-
warming, opening the door to Gywneth Paltrow, who's wearing an
expensive fur coat and has under her arm a big bowl of pasta salad
she's made herself.

"Hello, you must be Ben! You have the same name as one of
my ex-boyfriends. Unfortunately he had an alcohol problem," she
says.

I couldn't find the apartment right away, since I couldn't find my
map after my visit with Robert. I turned my room upside down, but
the search was in vain.

A young guy in a corduroy suit and sandals pointed the way for
me.

I was just about to knock when the door slowly opened and a frail hand groped for the handle, held onto it fast. A soft sniveling came from the apartment.

A man's voice yelled, "Now fuck off!"

The door was yanked wide open, and a woman with scraggly blonde hair flew into me, followed by a vaporous cloud of alcohol and cigarette smoke. I *just* caught her, and was looking into a pair of disturbed green eyes with widely dilated pupils. She began to cough; finally she freed herself from my arms and staggered away.

The zipper on her dress was open, and you could see red welts on her bare back. I watched her until the elevator door closed behind her.

"What're you lookin' at?"

Standing in the door of the apartment was a big, beefy kind of guy in jogging pants with close-cropped black hair; his lower lip was bleeding. He was pulling on a red jacket that featured two thumb-sized burn holes.

"I'm sorry, I've got the wrong door."

I turned and tried, through the power of my mind, to get the elevator back up here immediately.

"You've come about the room."

I've never had a problem with lying to get out of unpleasant situations. Not when I was caught in a physics test with a book on my lap; not when I came home from school one day and was met at the courtyard entrance by my mother waving a porn magazine she'd found under my bed. I always had a good story.

Yet now I was walking down the dark hallway of an even darker apartment, and heard the door being shut behind me and locked.

"Okay, let's get this over with," Jogging Suit said as he pushed past me, and I hoped he was talking about the room.

I followed him.

On the way, I took a peek at the kitchen, where a single candle provided a weak light. It stood on a table, in the middle of a bunch of empty beer bottles. On a nearby chair there was small orange TV from which soul music could be heard. The picture was bad.

Jogging Suit disappeared into the darkness.

Because I couldn't see anything, I took a step back. I called out to him, but didn't get any answer.

The TV was still playing music, without a picture.

I was considering whether I could find my way back to the door when a hand grabbed my arm.

"There's nothing to see here."

Jogging Suit pulled me into the darkness with him. He told me to wait, and let go of me. I heard him swear as he fumbled with something jangly.

Just a bit later his silhouette appeared against the window when he lifted the blinds, and more and more of the room gradually became visible.

We were standing in a big, empty room. At my feet was a stained green mattress, next to it was an empty beer bottle from which half the label had been scratched; a few other bottles lay strewn about the floor. The yellow wallpaper had begun to peel from the wall just above the baseboard, and I found a big patch of mildew next to the window.

"Five hundred a month, as advertised. Two months in advance. You have the money with you?"

Through the window next to him I could see the Hollywood sign up in the hills, a blue sky gleaming behind it—a beautiful view, and one that only strengthened my resolve to get out of that apartment as quickly as possible.

I was just trying to explain that, in principle, I thought it was really nice here, but that I had to think it over and I still had a couple other places to look at, when there was a knock at the door.

"Oh, and there's the next person to look at it," I trilled, relieved. "I'll get right out of here, I don't want to be in your way."

"Shut up!"

With that, he made his way past me and looked around the corner into the dark hallway. He stood there a moment and waited. A knock at the door again. Someone called out something.

"I'm sorry, I've really gotta get going. I'm seeing another apartment right after this in Santa M—"

"I said shut the fuck up!" he hissed.

His lower lip was still bleeding; he wiped his sleeve over his mouth and looked at the door again.

I was just beginning to wonder whether there was a fire escape outside the window when the door flew open with a loud crash. Jogging Suit beat it. A short time later I had the hard knee of a police officer in my back, who with one hand held my head facing the wall while with the other he gave me a rushed but well-aimed full-body frisk.

The first I see of James is the bouquet he's carrying as he turns the corner. I could do without the spiteful grin, but it's good to see him. He seems taller than I remembered him; he's outlined by a bright light, almost a bit blinding.

The guard with the pockmarked nose snatches the flowers from him and throws them on a table, which they slide over and land on the floor.

James is led to my cell. The guard mumbles something like: "Just fifteen minutes."

James takes me in his arms and whispers something to me I can't make out. Behind him the door is being bolted with a large security lock.

"Hey! No touching!" screams the pocked-nose of decency.

James lets go of me and turns to the door.

"I'm paying the bail. How much is it?"

The guard drops onto a chair and crosses his tattooed arms over his chest. First he looks at James, then me.

"Because it's you, ladies: ten thousand."

Shocked, I look from one to the other, till James puts his hand on my shoulder. He waves his other hand dismissively and says,

"No problem. I'll pay cash."

Someone banged on the bars of the jail cell with a stick, and brought me back to a Jamesless reality.

"Hey man, do you need a special invitation or are we gonna have to beat you?"

The guard stood in my cell looking at me impatiently. I wondered how long he had been standing there. Now I also noticed Jogging Suit, who was sitting next to me on the bench with his legs crossed, his eyes boring into me.

Somewhere the shrill cries of two women fighting over something could be heard; a male voice tried in vain to restore calm.

If only James would finally come. More likely Scott, since I had called him two hours ago when they locked me up. But maybe he would bring His Sweetness along.

I was hustled into a small room where there was a white table and two chairs. A black police officer in a pale blue shirt and red tie indicated that I should take a seat.

"You're here on vacation?"

"No, I'm trying to live here," I said.

"Trying?"

"Yeah, with different jobs."

I told him about the newspaper and about my new job with the theater, which earned a look of pity.

"And the reason why I—"

"How long have you known Thomas John Fisher?" interrupted the officer.

I wondered if he meant the guy who just a couple hours ago had gone from one to zero on the chart for my Favorite Potential Roommates, and from whose apartment I had thankfully been liberated.

"Please just answer the question. How long have you known him?"

"I don't know him at all."

"But you were in his apartment."

"Yeah, unfortunately," I said, subdued.

"What were you doing there?

"I was there to look at a room."

"You were going to move in with Thomas Fisher?"

"No."

"You just said you were in his apartment to look at a room."

"That's what I did."

It was apparent that the police officer didn't believe me.

Maybe I should have left the room and come back in, and we could have started the whole conversation over, but then came the next questions. Whether I used drugs. Whether I regularly got my drugs from Thomas John Fisher. And what I knew about his relationship with a certain Lucy Conner.

His questions were pretty confusing, if not exactly surprising, and after half an hour the guy had lost interest in me.

I was hustled back into my cell, where Jogging Suit awaited me.

"Thanks a lot, motherfucker! If you hadn't made such a big fucking scene at the apartment, she'd be moved out by now!"

"If you hadn't hit her and thrown her out of your apartment, she wouldn't have turned you in!" I thought, though I kept this thought to myself in the hope that it would increase my chances of leaving the cell in one piece rather than sliced.

"Ben, maybe it's a sign!" I heard Paula say.

"Guys're shooting you down one after the other, you can't find a decent apartment, and now this! Anyway, I don't know what you see in L.A. I mean: The place doesn't even have a bombed out memorial church."

Paula could be downright constructive at times.

I looked at the clock. My career as a drug dealer had officially begun about five hours ago.

My trial could be as early as tomorrow, after which I would in all probability have to serve a two-year sentence in the company of a poetry-writing serial killer who, before we go to sleep, reads to me from his works, in which colorful butterflies alight on verdant spring meadows. Afterwards he usually breaks into tears, and asks whether I could sleep in his bed, he feels so lonely.

At least that's his version.

Of course no one would believe me afterwards when I testified in court that he had forced me every night "to service him." (That was the wording suggested by my attorney; it's better than any technical term, and I can go into the details later, with a disgusted look on my face, if the judge or the lawyer so demands.)

I was hungry. I hadn't eaten since breakfast. The air was musty, like in the hotel room downtown, supplemented by the pungent smell of piss.

There was still no sign of Scott. He should have been here long ago.

Half an hour ago they brought in a new one, some guy who was just totally drunk and who regaled me with endless stories about his wife, who had left him. I felt sorry for him; just the same, I wished Jogging Suit would come back, who they were now questioning and who was probably telling them wild cock-and-bull stories to get back at me.

I heard steps. The pock-nosed guy came around the corner; behind him was Ramon, the Latino comedian who I had met at Scott and Pete's. He was wearing a light-colored suit and carried a briefcase under his arm, and seemed nearly personable in disguise. Finally Scott himself appeared, who called to me:

"Can't anyone let you out of their sight just for a day?"

A few minutes later I was sitting behind the two of them in the car, patiently and gratefully enduring the witticisms of my new friend, the comedian-lawyer.

Apparently during the interrogation Jogging Suit confirmed that he had never seen me before, and added that he never would have rented to a "fairy" like me anyway, not to mention doing business with me, since the very thought of the police scared the shit out of me.

"By the way, a certain Victor called," Scott told me. "He said something like: the woman was allergic to dog hair, so you can have the room if you still want it."

"Well then, little Paula-kins!" I thought. "And now what kind of sign is that?"

Ramon turned around to me.

"Should I have this Victor guy checked out before you end up with another pimp?"

I answered by smiling my benign Camilla-Parker-Bowles smile and thanked him politely.

So now I had two jobs and my own room, but something essential was still missing.

I found Matlock via the classified ads. He was a 1980, and therefore very inexpensive. It was love at first sight, and I took him right back home.

We took the test for a California driver's license together. It was shortly before Easter. Matlock and I waited on the line at the Department of Motor Vehicles; there were still two cars ahead of us.

Two testers were on duty. One was a mid-fiftyish woman in small round glasses and a plain suit, like the sweet little old aunt you take for a drive out into the country on a Sunday afternoon to set the world aright over coffee and cake and lament over how many calories you just shoved into yourself.

The other one had close-cropped hair and was wearing a baggy sweater over faded jeans. She was very tall, and came off as a gym teacher who'd retrained to become a butcher and who also worked weekends as an army instructor.

In strictly mathematical terms, she would have been the one to pass me, but when Matlock (a light blue-gray Volvo with brown leather seats) and I advanced to the starting position, she was just informing a young, red-faced, sweaty woman that she had failed the test, and went on her break.

Gratefully I showed the coffee-and-cake aunt my hand signals for left and right turns; nodding, she made notes on her checklist.

We were silent as I drove. I took in her instructions and confirmed them each time with a brief "Hmmm" before I turned, parked, or drove a short stretch in reverse.

After fifteen minutes we were reapproaching the DMV building, and I was going to have to turn left, which I also did admirably.

When I finally turned off the engine at her command, she asked me if I was trying to kill her. According to her, I should have waited for an approaching car to pass before I turned into the DMV parking lot, and that there was no way she could issue me a license.

I let her know that I considered there to have been a sufficiently safe distance between me and the other cars (which was true), and that nothing had even happened, the other guy didn't even honk.

She said that was no argument, and that I had failed the test.

That's unfair, I said back, and wouldn't accept her decision.

The coffee-and-cake aunt jumped out of the car and disappeared into the DMV building. Several minutes passed; nothing happened. I wondered whether I should follow her in or just drive home. Later on I could set up another appointment in a different part of the city.

Suddenly the door opened and the butcher lady stomped up to me. Instinctively I wanted to roll up the windows and lock all the doors.

"You don't want to accept my distinguished colleague's decision?" she bellowed at me.

"Well, uh … actually … no, I don't." I stammered.

"Are you ready to take the test over again?"

"If that's what has to be done."

"It's an exclusive exemption just for you, dear, because I'm having a good day. Now show me where the handbrake is."

Then it was the button for the rear window defroster, then the horn, and in all the excitement I confused the lever for the windshield wiper with the one for the low-beams.

I had to drive the same stretch again, which took nearly twice as long as the first time (the left turn in particular took way too much time), and half an hour later the butcher nearly broke my right hand as she congratulated me for passing my driver's test.

When I got home that night I fell into bed exhausted.

In my sleep I'm with Adam, we're going for a walk hand-in-hand along a lake outside Berlin.

Despite the cold wind, Adam's hands are warm; my ears, however, are glowing like the knobs in a pinball game.

A couple of birds circle above us, otherwise no one's around.

Now and then Adam kisses me on the mouth, which normally he doesn't like doing in public.

I don't know anymore who had the idea about the boat, probably me.

"Now show me where the handbrake is," he says as he sits down behind me.

I look for it in vain. I just can't find it.

We begin to row until Adam tells me I don't need my oar, I should throw it in the water and snuggle up to him, he's cold. I see the oar as it slowly drifts away and finally, with a gurgle, sinks. Then I let myself fall back into Adam's lap. But I fall on the hard bottom of the boat instead, Adam has disappeared. I hear a rippling sound and turn around.

With big, powerful strokes he's trying to swim for the shore, but he's not moving.

"Adam!" I call to him. "Where are you trying to go?"

"I don't know."

"But we're meeting Paula in an hour at that Italian place!"

"Sorry."

I lose sight of him.

There's a dull crash as the other boat rams me.

In the bow I see Brenda, who's wearing the butcher's baggy sweater and nervously lighting a cigarette.

"It would really mean a lot to Adam if you two could be friends," she calls to me, and begins to laugh loudly. Her boat begins to rock dangerously.

A faceless man is sitting at the oars. He's holding something in his hand and is waving it in front of my nose. It's a framed photo of me that used to hang in Adam's apartment.

"This belongs to you. Nobody there remembers you anymore."

The photo hits me in the head and then falls in the water.

I woke up and rubbed my temples.

"Hi, it's Ben."

"Uhhh …"

It was one of those I-hadn't-really-expected-to-hear-from-you-but-I'll-listen-to-what-you-have-to-say-as-long-as-it-doesn't-last-too-long-because-there's-a-long-list-of-men-who-want-to-go-out-with-me uhhh's.

"I was wondering whether by any chance you felt like going to the Abbey tonight. I have something to celebrate. Pete and Scott'll be there, too," I said.

"Nice idea. But I think I'm too tired to go out tonight. Maybe some other time."

I didn't believe a word James was saying.

"Okay. When?" I asked.

He blew into the receiver, and I hated him for that.

He should just say he doesn't want to see me. That he can picture a life without me. That he has no need for an attractive foreigner, an unassuming companion, a charming Christian (who left the church several years ago), a German drug dealer, a hater of ugly dogs, a savvy interior designer (he could find that out later), a youthful-looking jazz lover, a snappy columnist and a passionate lover who would massage his back black and blue before we fell asleep. Please!

I had two demanding jobs; my time was scarce. I couldn't split myself in two. James should just say that the next few days are all booked with important appointments—all of them unfortunately at night.

"Are you free tomorrow?" he asked.

I pressed my hand over the mouthpiece so he couldn't hear my cry for joy. Then I quickly coughed a couple times and took a deep breath.

"Sorry, I just have to check …"

I cleared my throat.

"No, unfortunately. And I'm afraid the whole week is booked. Just stupid appointments that I can't reschedule—always at night. But what do you say about next Wednesday?"

CHAPTER 8

You shouldn't get involved with a guy with a mustache, even when
—he can put the mustache to profitable use
—his boyfriend is away on business
—he deserves you

Every other person you meet in Los Angeles is either an actor or thinks he's one, usually a good one. You can tell them at a distance because of their blond highlights (the Americans haven't surpassed Europe in every area).

And living off of those who actually make money from acting—and here too there are the good ones, and then there's Kevin Costner—is a vast array of people: drug dealers, divorce lawyers, and above all, plastic surgeons. This group of professionals divides itself into three subgroups: those who can; those who can't; and those who make a living repairing what those who can't have done. These three groups are getting increasing competition from the so-called Botox doctors, who inject their clients, male and female, in the most unlikely places—beneath the eyes; in the brow; the palms of the hands; under the arms—with a paralyzing neurotoxin whose effects are temporary. This either keeps the clients young or at least stops them from sweating.

There's even a Botox doctor in Beverly Hills who serves bagels on special occasions when a new shipment of the neurotoxin comes in—with kind regards to his colleagues down the block who'll suck out all the fat later.

Not to be forgotten is that group of professionals euphemistically called journalists, who talk about the ones who can't or take pictures of the ones who are sweating like pigs.

George Clooney beats his girlfriend? Poor Julia Roberts had a miscarriage? Britney Spears has her tits operated on and afterwards has fatter knees?

It's wonderful: We make up a story; everything sells.

The heap of people making a heap of money every day with the tragic and not-so-tragic destinies of Hollywood is immeasurable, and they all have to wrestle with more or less ill-tempered editors in chief.

"I haven't yawned so much in a long time," Carstensen snapped on the other end of the line. "What's up with you? You don't even have a punch line! Did you even read my comments?"

The reason for the uproar was a story in my column about Jennifer Lopez. A costar who was supposed to have done a love scene with her went to pieces because he was so nervous.

Ms. Lopez comforted him, and asked if this was his first time in front of the camera. The man nodded, embarrassed, and Ms. Lopez told him that she was used to it, but that she met actors all the time who hadn't done it in front of the camera before.

That was it. No big story, forged perhaps from the *National Enquirer* or *People Magazine*. You read it and forget it immediately.

Carstensen was making such a scene you'd have thought he wanted to do a special supplement on it.

"Funny, up to now no one knew a thing about Jennifer Lopez's past in the porn industry."

That was his idea of a punch line, a good exit line, that he faxed to me and then recited to me again on the phone.

"So it has more bite, get it? A love scene with Jennifer Lopez in front of the camera—everybody thinks of porn right away and of that fucking hot ass of hers. Man!"

"Excuse me, boss, but I don't. Your punch line is tasteless."

"Now you're starting up with that again. The majority of our readers are men."

I have heard that text often before. I knew what was coming next.

"And the majority of them are, quite tastelessly, into this woman's ass. Could you maybe just try to put yourself in their position?"

I couldn't even try to position myself near Jennifer Lopez's ass. Carstensen was going to have to use his little porn line in his own column.

"Jackoff!" I said as I hung up the phone.

"Stupid jackoff!" he swore 6,000 miles away, and scratched his beard.

I was now briefly, as a journalist who made his living in entertainment, part of The Industry, and it simply couldn't be helped: Sooner or later you ran into all the other vultures.

So I got invited to a kind of exclusive group that met the first Tuesday of every month.

People who enjoy sitting around with colleagues who they don't like and to whom they have nothing to say and therefore sit around for hours talking about work go all the time.

I went once.

"Yesterday I was at the screening of the new Roberts film," said a slightly plump guy in brown jogging pants, an Austrian, as I seated myself at the table. What he really wanted to say was: He had seen a free preview of the new Julia Roberts film at the Foreign Press Association, of which he was a member. This association decides the annual awarding of the Golden Globes, the second most important award in American film and television. It also pays for decadent little niceties for its members, such as trips every year to numerous big film festivals (Australia, India, Cannes—the main thing is that it's far away), including hotel.

"A very promising beginning, but then it rapidly deteriorates. And the woman playing Douglas's wife—well, my mother could've pulled it off better."

"And she got a lifting because her eyes had sagged so much after her pregnancy," threw in an anorexic goat with blonde hair. She was a correspondent for one of the public radio shows. "But they weren't any better."

"It's just all too demented," said a little guy with glasses next to her; he worked as a cameraman for a TV production company.

"And did you read where this stalker who was bothering Nicole Kidman wants to run for president of the U.S. in three years. He said so on his website," the goat said.

"It just doesn't get any worse," said the man in the suit at the head of the table, and ordered a beer.

He had a handshake that was as greasy as the Hollywood column he wrote for a widely read German daily. It always ended with these sleazy sentences, like: "Dear Julia, was that really necessary?" or "Dear Harrison, shouldn't you keep in mind that you've got a sweet woman waiting for you at home?"

"How'd your interview with Tom go? Or has that not happened yet?" he was asked by the public radio goat.

"No, no, it was last weekend. It was very nice, but Tom and I …" the Oily One said and leaned back slowly, "… we've met a couple of times. A nice guy, really. Always very quick on the uptake, always funny."

"Have I ever told you …" the Austrian tried to reinsert himself into the conversation, "… how I ran into him in the bathroom at the Globes a couple of years ago. He was standing directly to my right, and then Spielberg comes in and stands on my left, and then they began to gossip. And how then Spielberg said, 'So what's up, are you doing the thing with James Ryan or not?"

"The last time you told this story, Hanks was on your left," laughed the guy in the glasses.

"It's a while ago. It has to have been five years ago," said the Austrian in jogging pants.

"No, the film came out in the summer of '98, it was more like four years ago," said the goat in her public radio voice.

"That can't be, because I wasn't at the Globes. I know that for a fact: In all the years I've only missed one, and that was because …"

It went on like this for hours.

But at least I accepted the invitation—and fled after twenty minutes.

I wanted to send Pete to it the next time so he could have his fun with the boys.

On the drive home I went past Adam's building; it was pretty much on the way. I had to make a little (in Los Angeles terms) detour, but I didn't care. The time I had originally allotted to spend with the vultures was now at my disposal.

My finger was already on the doorbell, but I hesitated.

"It would really mean a lot to Adam if you two could be friends."

Brenda's words were still on my mind ever since the boat dream. They made no sense. Competing memories emerged from the past and raised objections.

"Can you really imagine, little guy, watching the sun set here all the time instead of in Germany? Presuming I don't always have to be with you."

Adam knew how to make romantic ideas sound unromantic, so that you never knew whether to take him seriously.

We spent a weekend at Joshua Tree, where we visited the national park during the day. It was dark in our bungalow, and I had just about fallen asleep when suddenly he took my hand and asked in his roundabout way whether I wanted to move to Los Angeles to be with him.

My hand was trembling. Had I already rung the bell? I held my breath and waited.

A complete refrain of "Close to You" later, nothing had happened.

Maybe he's just not home, I thought. His white pickup was nowhere to be seen, but he usually parked it in the underground garage.

I decided to go. It certainly wasn't a good idea, popping up here unannounced. Adam hated surprise visits.

I rang the bell.

Sweat gathered beneath my armpits, my throat was dry, like it was that stifling day at Joshua Tree National Park when we drank up our entire water supply within two hours.

"You're sucking this stuff down like it's a martini," Adam said, and put the empty bottle back in his backpack.

No one buzzed me in; apparently there really was no one home. I rang one more time and took a couple steps back.

A small bird was sitting on Adam's windowsill, cleaning its feathers. Behind the pane of glass I saw a man with conspicuously large teeth, who ducked away with a start when he saw me looking.

Paula didn't have a clue.

"So what does that prove?" she said, though the man in the window proved everything. After all, he had insinuated himself into the boat dream earlier. Now he had gotten a face. And teeth.

"And why do you still want to stay there now that you've got the goods on Adam?"

But things were going well for me in Los Angeles. I had a new home. I even had an entire apartment to myself (and an ugly dog, which I had taken for a short walk after nightfall). Robert had a business dinner.

And tomorrow I was getting together with James.

That is, if we were still on. We hadn't been in touch since our phone conversation. Maybe he had forgotten our date. Or could he possibly be waiting for me to call him?

"Hi, did you really forget our dinner date or are you just not calling because you can do whatever you want?"

Or had he met someone?

That was the basic advantage of boring cities like Karlsruhe or Hildesheim. The danger of losing a great guy in the blink of an eye to another great guy wasn't so great in places like that (not that many great guys). On the other hand, James didn't speak a word of German, he would be way too fixated on me there, and it wouldn't be good for our relationship.

I put the dirty dishes from the weekend into the dishwasher. Afterwards I sat in front of the TV with a bottle of beer and beamed myself across the world.

On "Who Wants to Be a Millionaire?" a shaky woman from Connecticut was about to crash and burn on the $1,000 question because she was declaring Earth to be the center of the solar system.

The M.C., whose name I could never remember, Regis Somethingorother, who had the shit-eating demeanor of a savings and loan clerk—rather, a retired savings and loan clerk—repeated the question two times, and said the words "solar system" particularly slowly, yet to no avail. The camera showed her fat, sweating husband in close-up, his chunky hands balled into fists he was crossing his fingers so hard. You could see the tension in his face, as well as his unbounded love for his wife.

She locked in "Earth."

The camera panned back to her husband: an understanding, sympathetic and affectionate smile that didn't seem to be from this solar system. And it was genuine; after all, this was presumably the guy's first and last time on television.

I felt miserable.

Paula wouldn't have understood, so I called Scott. As far as I knew, Pete was serving cold champagne and tomato juice somewhere up in the air between Los Angeles and Caracas. Scott would be alone.

"Sun speaking. Sun to Earth?"

"Did you see that guy?"

"The fat one? Do you like him?"

I could have really done without Scott's cynicism.

"Could we just have a serious conversation for once?" I asked, irritated.

He was silent.

"I mean: what was that?"

"That was a pretty embarrassing little performance."

"Yeah, but what would you do if Pete embarrassed himself in front of the whole world because he didn't know the simplest things?"

"Pete doesn't know the simplest things. But he also doesn't not know them on TV—though he'd have a really good chance if they only asked him questions about Madonna," he said.

"But what do you think? Would you be able to smile affectionately and declare your love for him? I saw you at dinner last week, and you looked as if you were about to wring his neck."

Scott hesitated a moment before he answered.

"You've had relationships yourself, Ben."

I didn't like the way the word "had" sounded.

"That's not an answer."

"I think it is," Scott said in a tone that indicated he'd like to end the discussion at this point.

"You'd never see me with a smile like that," I continued trying.

"Are you jealous?" he asked.

I sighed softly, then said:

"I wish you were here."

He turned his glass on the napkin for the thirty-seventh time and gazed into the candlelight. He stroked the tablecloth, lost in thought.

Above him was a starry sky; jazz played softly in the background intermingled with a mishmash of the conversations of a dozen other diners, but he didn't really take them in.

Then the waiter came, exchanged a few words with him and disappeared again.

He seemed pensive, maybe even sad, you couldn't really tell. Now and again he looked at his watch and picked at his right ear.

The woman at the next table turned to him and asked if it would bother him if she smoked. He gave a friendly smile and shook his head.

What a question when you're sitting outside! But so California.

When you went near his table, you could smell him (despite the cloud of nicotine at the next table, the winds were favorable). It was a pleasant, by no means obtrusive scent. On his throat, just under his chin, he had tiny cut, the kind you get from shaving. Otherwise he came off as very well-groomed, the well-groomed look that people have when they're waiting for a lover, male or female. Could people tell which he was waiting for just by looking at him? Was he perhaps *too* well-groomed? Does the way he holds his glass betray something about him?

All the other diners were looking over at him. Something about him wasn't right, you could feel it. Some began to whisper. It was becoming more and more apparent, like adding one plus one.

There! He looked at his watch again! Then he lifted his eyebrows, sighed, and wiped his mouth. He'd been stood up, all his showering and shaving had been for naught.

What was he going to do? the people wondered.

Did he have tears in his eyes or rage in his gut?

How long would he keep waiting?

And what was that playing in the background, that kitschy song with the woman singing about birds and stars falling from the sky?

Just like me
They long to be
Close to you

A tall, good-looking man appeared at his table, spoke briefly with him, and sat down. The tension in him dropped away, you could just about hear it, like in those ads a while ago where people eating yoghurt with too much fat and calories crashed through the floor in their chair.

"Oops!" the other guests in the restaurant now thought, "This is the one he was waiting for. He must be a great guy if he knows someone like that. He must be really funny, smart, and charming, too. What a great couple!"

"Sorry," James said. "I couldn't get away from the gym any earlier. Then I got stuck in traffic. They're filming again down on Sunset. I hope you haven't been waiting long."

"No problem, I just got here."

He looked fabulous in his tight white sweater, his hair still wet from the shower, and he was smiling broadly at me.

"I like it outside here. Have you ever been here during the day?"

I shook my head, and was astonished when he pulled the table-cloth back and showed me all the cigarette burns in the wood surface of the table.

"These pigs. Aren't there any ashtrays here?"

"That's not from people putting out their cigarettes. That's what I thought, too, the first time I came here. But it's from the sun. When its rays come through the glasses during the day, it can actually start a fire. That's why they don't put cloths on the table during the day; otherwise the fabric would ignite.

He covered up the burn holes again and looked at me.

"You don't come to work out anymore. Obviously you didn't like it."

"No, it was great. I just haven't had the time," I lied.

"That's one of the most common excuses. And also the worst."

"Okay, let's just say that the next time I feel the need to do penance for my numerous sins and I want to spend another three days on the couch without being able to bend my arms, I'll stop by."

The waitress came and glowingly took our order.

"Hi, my name's Tina, and I will be your waitress."

While James dealt with what dressing he wanted for his salad, I pictured him bringing me coffee and homemade cake in bed—and ice cubes for him to use on my swollen arms.

"How was your day?" he asked when Tina, our waitress, had left. Under the table he'd started up with his foot-tapping thing. The water in my glass was getting stormy.

I tried to ignore it, and shared a bit of gossip from my humble day job, threw in a handy fitness tip from Julia Roberts (jumping rope four times a week, always exactly at 8:00 in the morning—no wonder men can never stay around this woman for long), and finally a recent statistic: Oscar winners live four years longer than those merely nominated. Which raises the justifiable question as to how much higher the life expectancy for a prize-winning, rope-jumping Erin Brockovich portrayer must be.

Somehow this got James talking about the disproportionately lower life expectancy of squirrels in Surprise Valley, where he grew up, northeast of San Francisco. He was much more relaxed than he was that night at Scott and Pete's; he talked about himself more. A good sign. I was happy.

"Those little things are real pests. In March there's always a big squirrel hunt back home; people come from all over the country for it. And their goal is to shoot at least one hundred per day," he said.

In one episode of *Sex and the City*, Carrie Bradshaw remarks quite aptly that squirrels—or, to be fair, the fat American version of them that repulsed Carrie so—are actually nothing more than rats in nicer outfits.

"Not that I'm particularly sympathetic to fat little American squirrels, but do they really have to execute them?" Proud of having raised the issue of the death penalty, I made a critical face.

"Sometimes animal rights people come and protest that we shoot all these little animals," he said, unmoved. "But then my Dad tells them how we have to shoot a horse when it breaks its leg stepping into a hole. But more than anything, they ruin the crops."

"Have you shot one yourself?"

"A horse? No," he replied.

I decided to elegantly change the subject, and looked into his dreamy green eyes.

"Do you like the Carpenters?"

"My grandmother had one of their cassettes; it was horrible, it would just go on and on. She'd listen to it every time I came to visit her. But she's already a bit off. Why?"

"Great!" I thought, "At least my taste in music is shared by a senile old lady."

I drank some water. I'd have rather had wine, but I wasn't sure what my horrifically healthy, salad-eating companion would think of it. I was happy enough that I wasn't craving a cigarette.

"I just happened to hear a song by them on the radio today," I said, after having listened to "Close to You" as I got ready for the evening. "It's just too beautiful for words and I had never heard it in Germany."

"Sing some."

I preferred reciting a passage.

"On the day that you were born
The angels got together
And decided to create a dream come true.

"Kitschy, huh?"

"But very pretty. Did you know that Burt Bacharach wrote that?"

If only Adam could have heard that! I thought. So there was some-one besides me who understood something about good music.

"Of course. Though I didn't know until three years ago who Burt Bacharach was," I said.

"And how did that happen?"

"I saw *Austin Powers*. Burt Bacharach was in it for a bit."

"My favorite movie," James said.

"No, mine," I said, and pushed my hand toward the center of the table.

He smiled and touched my hand briefly with his fingertips.

"And the sequel is your president's favorite movie," I said and wanted to kiss James so badly.

"Says who?" he said.

"Bush, your president. You could almost like the guy for that, couldn't you?"

We went on about the first movie's soundtrack a bit, in which there were two Burt Bacharach songs, and kept looking into each other's eyes. I said we couldn't kiss Mike Myers' feet enough for making those movies.

"You into that?" he asked.

I still had to get him used to not taking me literally, so I deflected him by telling a quick story about Paula.

It was a great evening, and we laughed a lot.

As we were leaving, we even spotted Liz Hurley (in Los Angeles you can't be picky about which celebrities you run into). She was sitting across from a tall, almost entirely white-haired man; the two of them had apparently just arrived, and their faces were burrowed in their menus. Yet when a little, bent-over old lady showed up at their table apparently looking for an autograph, Hurley unsheathed one of her icy smiles.

We had to laugh at the coincidence of just having talked about the Austin Powers movie and then running into Liz Hurley, who plays an agent in the film and has to kiss the yellow-toothed Mike Myers.

James's apartment was small. A pair of shoes was lying around on the floor, books, and a copy of *Men's Health* in which the cover article was "Are You Better Than Average? The Big Test", a quiz about impotence and an advice columnist who in the American edition was appropriately named Dr. Schwanz, which is "cock" in German.

"Dear Dr. Schwanz," I thought as James disappeared into the bathroom. "I'm afraid I like this guy. And if there's anything that can be done to stop it—please don't tell me."

There's this scene in *Thelma and Louise* where the women spend the night in a motel and Geena Davis spends the night with Brad Pitt.

When she appears at breakfast the next morning, she's beautiful and is beaming this amazing smile.

I considered her a terrific actress because of this, even after seeing *Cutthroat Island*. But when I looked in the mirror after spending the night with James, I knew: Geena Davis had actually slept with Brad Pitt.

At the Starbucks where I have my daily latte macchiato prepared, I was received like a prince. The two chess players outside by the entrance forgot their strategies, and the guy with the headphones, who till now had been in the lead, lost his queen on the next move.

In just the five-minute walk it took me to get there, the city of Los Angeles recorded the greatest number of rear-end collisions in its 166-year history (and on dry streets yet, since it hadn't rained for weeks): Everybody was craning their neck to see me, thinking, "Hey now, there's a guy who really got some last night!"

James's body was genuinely worthy of worship, and I couldn't wait to worship it again.

My column the next day was a song of praise to love, and covered the new old happiness of Alec Baldwin (the pudgy guy in the Fred Segal store) and Kim Basinger, who had very recently moved back in together. But Diane Keaton complained in an interview that she had only had brief episodes of being in love, and that she no longer believed in finding the right man. "Hey!" I screamed at her, "Elizabeth Taylor's old enough to be your mother, and you don't see her making a big deal out of it; she just gets married every now and then."

(The next day I got my first fan e-mail from a reader who was so old that she possibly could have been Elizabeth Taylor's mother, and she was infinitely grateful because my writing had given her "a new lease on life and love." This is why I love my job.)

In the afternoon I was back sitting at the theater writing copy for a new Tennessee Williams adaptation that had been in rehearsal for weeks, and then later sold a slew of tickets for the evening performance. Currently playing was a modern staging of *Arsenic and Old Lace*.

I gave every customer my Geena Davis smile and counted the hours until I would see James again that evening.

"You look as if you've either had incredible sex or that Christmas and your birthday both fell on the same day today," Roshumba, one of the nicer actresses, whispered to me before she went backstage.

"If you mean my eighteenth birthday," I yelled after her, "then it's even better!"

After the performance had begun, I slipped into the theater. It was nearly sold out, which for the second performance after the opening wasn't anything special.

"You've never seen *Arsenic and Old Lace* like this!" I had written in the press release, knowing that most people also certainly didn't want to see one like this.

The director, a woman, had turned the two sweet little old aunts of the original into a pair of lesbian lovers (Roshumba played the good-natured Martha; they'd stuck her in denim overalls; Abby, her girlfriend, wore an army camouflage outfit). Together they poisoned a total of twelve HIV-infected men, who Teddy, their son, had to bury in the basement. Teddy wasn't entirely sane, and thought he was nurse Carol Hathaway from the series *ER*.

When I tried to cram myself into the seat next to a very fat woman (somewhere near where Adam and I had sat for the Callas piece—but I hardly thought of that anymore), the mothers had just disclosed to Teddy that there had been a new death.

"My word!" said the Nurse Hathaway-wannabe, "another victim of yellow fever!"

The audience laughed. The fat woman next to me began to gasp because she couldn't catch her breath.

Later the two lesbians tell their best friend Mortimer (magnificently played in the film by Cary Grant, Gavin had the role here, which the director had expanded to make him a sperm donor as well; so Gavin was Teddy's biological father) as a matter of course about the twelve dead people in the basement who, as they literally put it, they "wanted to bring closer to God."

"Hmm, twelve. Well …" Gavin said, not quite understanding the seriousness of the situation.

"TWELVE!!!" he cried suddenly, tussled his hair, and for a second looked even more deranged than Teddy in his *ER* mode.

It was a very funny scene, and Gavin got the most enthusiastic applause I had yet heard as I left the theater to drive over to James's.

Whose body was no less adorable than it had been when I left it the night before. Maybe he'd ask me to stay the night this time, and we could have breakfast together the next morning. In my mind I loaded up a plate of croissants, pancakes with syrup, and yellow beans in a thick sauce.

"Dear Dr. Schwanz, since I had sex with this personal trainer, I've had strange cravings. Certainly I'm not pregnant already!"

He kept his feet still in bed—or in any case, he didn't tap them (a clear sign, of my calming influence). My head lay quite comfortably on his chest, on which not a single hair grew—but that didn't bother me. I had my own hair, even if there wasn't much of it.

I was just counting the hairs below his bellybutton when the telephone rang. I was up to twelve. ("Hmm, twelve. Well…")

My head hit the mattress as James got up and pulled on his underwear. He left the room with the telephone. I rolled over onto my stomach and sniffed his pillow.

After five minutes I got up and looked out the window. It was a little before midnight. Outside someone got in his car and drove away. A lot of lights were still burning in the buildings across the street: some people were watching TV, others had their blinds closed and were doing god-knows-what.

After yet another five minutes I went into the living room and inspected his CD collection.

Then I went to the bathroom.

On the way, I heard James in the kitchen saying there was nothing to tell. "Great," I thought, "he'll be right back."

Unfortunately I realized in the bathroom that my breath could have anaesthetized an entire suite of operating rooms. I rinsed my mouth out, and wondered why there were so many toothbrushes. Why would someone need three of them when, like most Americans, he only has twenty-eight teeth?

Then I wanted to wash my feet in the small sink and nearly lost my balance trying. At the end I tried to make something of my tousled hair, but finally gave up.

"Where were you so long?" James would ask when I slipped right back into bed.

But instead when I opened the bathroom door, I heard him saying again that there was nothing to tell. And, after a slight pause: "I'm sorry."

I remained standing where I was and controlled my breathing yet again.

James repeated himself and apologized at irregular intervals. In between, he once said, "Nobody … No, nobody."

There aren't particularly a lot of explanations for this type of conversation. Or I just didn't think what they might be.

I went quietly back into the bedroom and got dressed. Slowly at first, then I started hurrying. James had been on the phone already for more than twenty minutes.

When I came back to the kitchen, the door was shut.

CHAPTER 9

You should never sleep with a stranger who's in a committed relationship, unless:
—he calls and promises that he's breaking up with his boyfriend immediately to spend the rest of his life with you
—he calls and promises that he's breaking up with his boyfriend
—he calls

I couldn't get out of James's apartment so easily.

Of course, I was physically and mentally capable of it; I just didn't want to.

As I got my stuff together and buttoned my shirt, I thought about the various ways of making a gracious exit …

I go quietly to the kitchen and carefully turn the door handle.

James is pacing back and forth, saying over and over that there's nothing to tell. Now and then he shifts the receiver to his other ear. He stops when he sees me standing in the door and makes an apologetic gesture.

I yell very loudly:

"Had a great time with you, James! I'm heading out now."

I picture his boyfriend on the other end of the line, his eyes and mouth gaping—I'm sure he has enormous teeth.

In another scenario I walk up to him slowly, stand before him, quite close, and look him right in the eye.

First he looks down at the floor, but becomes nervous and looks back up at me again. He begins to shake his head cautiously as he says "Nobody" into the receiver two times, one right after the other.

I kneel on the floor and quickly yank his underwear down.

When he tries to turn away, I hold him fast by the hips. He tries to push my head away, which makes him lose his balance, but he catches himself on the table. A glass falls to the floor and shatters.

Now he lets me do as I please, even closes his eyes and seems to enjoy it. Then I stand up and leave.

In another scenario I combine these ideas.

Version 4:

I stand at the closed door just for the briefest moment, and run back into the living room. I grab a pen and in big letters I write on the cover of *Men's Health*, "Call me!" I put the magazine on his pillow and slip out of the apartment.

Once on the street, I noticed how angry I was. Less at James than at myself, but far more at someone else.

As soon as I got home I grabbed the phone.

It took a while for someone to answer.

"Thanks for the warning," I said.

Pete wasn't entirely awake, which you couldn't really begrudge him at one in the morning.

"Ohmygod, what happened?"

"You knew that James had a boyfriend, didn't you."

"Oh, he told you, hon?"

"Not directly."

"Maybe just for a change you should look for someone who's available. Someone you could actually be with, you know? What is that saying, that puts it so nicely: "Pain is a warning that something's wrong."

Paula congratulated me on my pending departure.

"Now will you finally come back to Berlin? We've already had two days of sunlight this month. You'd be amazed!"

"You act as if I had only been staying here because of James," I said.

"Let me just reconstruct this a bit," she said. "You had that accident the day you were originally going to leave. When you called me about these people, you said something like, 'Not interested anymore, shitty city, I'm outta here.' Two days later you were looking for a room and a job in the same shitty city. What the hell happened in between?"

Paula wasn't saying that to be mean. She missed me. And I missed her, and those evenings with her when we'd wrap ourselves up in blankets and read to each other out of previous years' horoscopes and try to figure out what we did wrong since we still hadn't met the man of our dreams and instead were meeting the Ass of the Month or the Bore of the Week.

I had pulled back the past couple years out of consideration for Adam, but next year I was going to be fully on board again.

Sometimes we got drunk with our friend Martina and tried to utter worldly wisdom with our mouths full and the other one would have to guess what it was.

Or we'd watch bad movies in fast forward, always a few per evening, and then think up plots and tragic endings. *Spice World* is the only one that stumped us.

I never had so much fun with a man as I had with Paula, and I was happy it never occurred to us (or to me, at least) to re-enact with her the scene from *The Next Best Thing* in which Madonna sleeps with her best and gayest friend Rupert Everett and threatens to destroy their friendship—by the way, also one of our fast-forwards.

Still, I didn't want to go back. Later maybe; maybe not at all; not at the moment at any rate.

Paula could say as much as she wants that happy endings only exist in Hollywood.

The plan was: Don't give up.

The plan was open to various interpretations. The most favorable went:

Ben is tough; he's not going to let himself be beaten down by a few strokes of fate. He has something in his sights, and nothing and no one is going to keep him from it.

Gavin, the only person in L.A. who was surprised by my James story, was a proponent of this thesis and convinced me, as a way to get my mind off it, to go out the next night with a few friends and colleagues to Ultra Suede (the silly man who wanted to interview Nicole Kidman and the Pope fortunately wasn't among them; the two of them had broken up).

Fridays, a DJ whipped up an adorable party with old records from the 90s. It was practically the same songs every week, and after a couple times you even knew the playlist. It was like good sex with someone you'd known a long time. It didn't surprise you anymore, but you were also very rarely disappointed.

In the club next door there was a house party, which personally didn't tempt me in the least since the place was five times as big and you had to wait in line nearly an hour (not because the place was so packed inside, but because a long line outside looks impressive and attracts other customers) just to have yourself blasted with music that was twice as loud—and for twenty dollars.

Admittedly, it's all a matter of faith once you reach a certain age. You can submit to whatever the musical taste of the moment is, you can enjoy pulling off your way-too-tight-anyway T-shirt on the dance floor (when I was a little kid, I thought it was great to run through the pedestrian mall with my shirt off in summer when it was hot) and, despite your splendidly clean-shaven chest, feel older than you actually are among all the twenty-somethings.

Or you can face up to your own past, dancing to music you didn't have the heart to officially consider good back in the day, keep your undershirt on (since you couldn't dance topless at the

Ultra Suede), and beam yourself back to a time when you actually were younger.

Besides, here you didn't have to wait more than fifteen minutes to get in, the advantage of which was that you didn't want to sit down first thing you got in because your feet hurt so much from standing forever in line. Have I mentioned that I'm no longer seventeen?

I stood at the bar with Gavin and a director from the theater. We drank Cosmos (they didn't serve martinis here, a real drawback) and talked trash about the woman in dark blue leggings and white sneakers who was bouncing around the still-empty dance floor. Her dancing style, combined with her outfit, reminded me of the open house at our school gym when different jazz groups consisting of fifteen women each and at least one slut demonstrated their choreography to "Flashdance" or "Saddle Up": step right; step left; clap your hands twice; repeat from the beginning.

Another highlight was the rewarding performance by a dark-haired guy in a turquoise headscarf and black Russian shirt that was unbuttoned so far down that it slipped off his left shoulder while he was dancing—and he just left it. This guy, a tragically unrecognized flamenco talent, clapped along to every song (even "Living on a Prayer" by Bon Jovi), and only allowed himself a break when he got a drink at the bar, which he always held in both hands to cool his palms. He was Gavin's favorite.

"Clearly a victim of yellow fever," he said, alluding to the scene from *Arsenic and Old Lace*.

Thus we whiled away the time till we ourselves went out on the dance floor and became objects of general ridicule.

That was where I brought the Gentleman Groper to his attention. A not unattractive medium-sized guy with dark hair and a white shirt that he wore completely open. He was very buff and moderately hairy. I acted as if I had just seen him for the first time.

"He's here a lot," Gavin said. "And every time he's totally blotto. Watch what he does."

At first glance it looked like dancing, but it was actually more a rhythmic stroll through the club, which had gotten quite crowded in the meantime. He'd stop in front of various people and dance up to them, somewhere in the process either putting his arm against their hip or letting his hands wander over their torso. Sometimes he'd quickly grab a guy in the crotch, push his hand in the guy's pants for a few seconds, maybe move it around a little and then pull it out again. Then he'd continue his little stroll.

"I always think he's trying to see who's got the biggest cock," Gavin said.

"But he doesn't stay by anyone more than a few seconds. And hardly anyone resists. Sometimes he'll even let himself be groped, but just for a little bit. And he goes back to some guys a second time, but I think that's because he's so drunk and can't remember."

Just then the Gentleman Groper stood behind him and pushed his hand around his hips, but Gavin turned around, smiled at him and pushed him away. The Groper withdrew without protest, and found his next victim a few yards away.

"And how long does it take for him to decide on someone?" I asked.

"That's just it. He always goes home alone."

I watched him for a bit.

When at 2:00 a.m. the announcement "Last call for alcohol!" sounded, I'd lost sight of him.

You can argue whether someone is basically happier going back to a big, empty bed when he's enjoyed at least some kind of bodily contact beforehand, or whether in the end he's more content cuddling through the night with the cold satisfaction that he's resisted questionable temptations and not been easy pickings.

Fiddling around with other people's nipples or zippers on California dance floors is, by the way, nothing special. People have to compensate for the banned back rooms in this country somehow.

(In Cape Town, the patrons of gay bars turn the bathrooms into back rooms by unscrewing the light bulbs or just by quickly smashing them. But the well-brought-up Californians would never do something like that.)

At any rate, the next day no one would mention it anymore, and you could take comfort in your latte (macchiato) that you'd never do such a stupid thing again and be at peace until the next temptation—till you met the brother of the Gentleman Groper, the guy in the sauna or the hitchhiker playing his mischief along Santa Monica Boulevard.

How it came about and with whom, whether in the end you even allowed it—it was always wrong.

That night I fell into bed and thought of James.

The plan was: Don't give up.

And, less favorably interpreted, that meant: Don't give up James. More nicely put: Don't give up hope, keep looking forward. Put setbacks behind you and keep struggling.

Paula hit on an even less favorable interpretation.

"Who is it you're trying to prove something to?" she asked again, and then: "Happy endings exist only in Hollywood."

"But Paula, I *am* in Hollywood."

CHAPTER 10

Don't trust anyone who promises he'll give you a job if you have sex with him, unless:
—it's a really good job
—the sex is really good and
—he keeps his promise

"I used to go to parties like that a lot!" Pete said blithely when we met for breakfast in Los Feliz.

The night before I'd had a dream about a strange party where all the guests were totally naked. But I couldn't identify their gender, like on those sex websites on the Internet where you have to give your credit card number first before the site's unlocked to you. In a panic I clasped the towel I was wearing around my hips. I was afraid of losing it and becoming like them. They danced and smoked and rubbed their bodies rhythmically against each other.

The whole night I was looking for Adam. We had a date, but I couldn't find him among all the people. In the morning I spent a long time puzzling over what the message of the dream might be, and the only thing Pete had to say about it was:

"I used to go to parties like that a lot!"

It was just noon, but already overcast, a typical hazy June day in L.A., known locally as "June gloom." We were sitting outside.

Pete had recently dyed his hair. It shimmered with a bluish tint, and made him seem paler than he was. Even the German chancellor's tint job is more convincing.

"That was … uhhh … a few years ago already. We hadn't met yet, darling."

Apparently he had let some cat out of the bag because he reached over and patted Scott on his hairy forearm. But only briefly, because Scott pulled it away, crossed his arms, and said:

"If I might quote your special girlfriend here: Once you put your hand in the flame, you can never be the same."

"Ooops, I didn't know we couldn't talk about sex!" Pete followed suit with another Madonna song and looked at me as if he expected some kind of support.

"It was even in Berlin, honey. Everyone naked, you know? It wasn't as bad as I had expected, and you didn't have to do anything if you didn't want to."

Berlin had more museums than Los Angeles had Starbucks. You had to visit one of the castles—in a pinch, you can do the Pfaueninsel, which Friedrich Wilhelm II had built so he had someplace to boff the Countess Lichtenau. For all I cared, Pete could have had his picture taken at the East Side Gallery or paid twelve dollars for a glass of champagne at the top of the TV tower at Alexanderplatz, but he was running around to naked dance parties!

"Well, then," I said, "you've been to a party like that. I'm dreaming about one. But why?"

Scott looked at me darkly.

"You just answered your own question."

Pete looked questioningly from Scott to me like someone who didn't get a joke.

I regretted having told Scott my dream, and began stirring my coffee aimlessly.

In front of us a man tied two big Labradors, one black, the other yellow, to a lamppost and disappeared into a restaurant.

Pete took his hand from Scott's arm and copiously wiped a few crumbs from the corners of his mouth.

"By the way, James came over yesterday for lunch."

I regretted telling Pete about my dream. Now that I had my own room and represented no direct threat to his relationship when he was away, he tried on a regular basis to pour salt on my wounds.

I hadn't seen James for over a week, and what wouldn't I have given to know that he had been over for lunch yesterday or which socks he had worn.

Instead I said:

"You think the sun'll come out again later? I haven't been to the beach in a while."

A woman was standing in front of our table talking to the two dogs. She rubbed them on their necks, their throats, paid them compliments; then she squatted in front of them.

The Labs were thrilled.

"Which one of you beauties wants to give me a kiss?"

The black one wanted to. He licked her across the face and a couple of times on her mouth, which she was sticking out at him while she cooed and muttered with pleasure. A cute young Latino guy at the next table was also observing the scene and dropped a piece of silverware on his plate, catapulting a piece of his burger onto the ground. The woman picked up the piece of meat, took it between her teeth and held it out to the black Lab. He ran his soggy tongue carefully over her lips and lapped up the gift.

"Good boy!" the woman rejoiced, and hugged the poor dog.

"And now who wants to give Mommy a kiss?"

Now it was the yellow Lab's turn to suffer.

The guy at the neighboring table jumped up, held both his hands before his mouth, and ran into the restaurant. As he ran in, he nearly collided with the owner of the dogs, who had just come out with a small white paper bag and a paper cup of coffee.

The woman stood up and wished the man and his dogs a good day. She walked over a few steps to a man who was leaning against a palm tree, apparently waiting for her, and threw her arms around his neck.

"I wonder what she would've done with those dogs if the guy hadn't gotten out here in time," Pete said.

Scott shook his head.

"If I caught someone doing that with the cats, I'd shoot him."

"Didn't Liz Taylor once say that she'd always much rather be around horses and dogs? Speaking of which, hon: Did I ever tell you the story about when I was in the sex shop in San Fran? There's this special video section, ohmygod! Behind this big black lacquered curtain, and that's where you found all the really disgusting stuff like ..."

I was holding the spoon in my hand that I'd been stirring my coffee with the past few minutes, and looked at the two of them.

"Okay, can we maybe just talk a little bit about James?"

Saturday nights are the worst nights for going out.

No, seriously.

People who should otherwise have never left the suburbs are always bumping into you at overcrowded clubs, and you spill your melon martini for which you've paid half your legal estate and are already regretting that you made your annual contribution to Alcoholics Anonymous yesterday.

When dancing, you thoughtfully forego particularly expressive gestures so that no one gets one of your splayed fingers stuck in his eye or has his foot stepped on, and then get slammed in the back by two babes who absolutely have to discofox to Britney Spears.

Everyone's totally uptight and has this angry look.

You absolutely have to enjoy yourself and even more absolutely you have to meet someone, and if you go home with only one new telephone number (or all alone), then the evening has been for naught.

And if you see a tall guy with dark hair who you like, then you immediately see the next one, and then another one, and look at that one, that guy at the bar, no, not the one in the cowboy hat, next to him, the black guy with the goatee, isn't he pretty good, too?

Who can make the right decision in such a situation? Who gets turned down and who gets the telephone number? And where has the tall dark-haired guy gone off to, and also: is the goatee guy back there in that dark corner making out with the cowboy hat?!

And so you plod back home alone, and lie in bed and, because you can't sleep, count guys instead of sheep. The ones you couldn't bring yourself to talk to, and the ones who landed in the problem zone on the walk-past. And because you're still not tired, now you even start counting the men you idled a few years of your life away with, and even those you loved but who suddenly developed a taste for men with big teeth, and you don't leave out the ones with adorable bodies, the ones with whom you have frighteningly good sex, but nothing more can happen with them because they're stuck in some fucking relationship.

That's why Saturday nights are the absolutely worst nights to go out.

I spared myself the whole thing. I stayed home, emptied the dishwasher (Robert must have forgotten), and spent the evening with the Carpenters. Reading the booklet that came with the CD, I saw that my birthday fell within the four weeks that "Close to You" was at the top of the American charts. I bemoaned the premature death of Karen Carpenter, the singer who had died at the age of thirty-three as a result of anorexia; and then, shifting gears, bemoaned the premature departure of Adam and James from my life.

There was nothing new to report about James, which didn't keep Pete from taking a half hour doing so.

James was doing well, he looked good, as he always did, and was behaving as he always did, you know (all things which I didn't want to hear).

No, not a word about his boyfriend.

No, he hadn't asked about me.

No, also hadn't said hello.

Yes, Pete was sure.

Yes, absolutely sure, honey.

"You know, Madonna is right: If you have to ask for something more than once or twice, it wasn't yours in the first place."

I lay on my bed and, when I wasn't either staring holes into the ceiling or fixating on images of James, I was looking at the clock in the hope that time would pass a little more quickly. Or that someone might call.

9:47. But that's what time it was the last time I looked at the clock. I ran into the kitchen to find out what time it really was, since my clock must have stopped.

9:48. Apparently some big technical snafu that affected the entire house.

I found a big container of ice cream in the fridge, which I took back to bed with me. Pralines and cream: mmmmmm!

9:56. I've been forsaken by all my friends.

Scott and Pete hadn't been in touch since we met for breakfast, those double-crossers.

Even Paula didn't call. Okay fine, with the time difference it was only 7:00 a.m. in Germany, but maybe there the clocks were functioning glitch-free and Paula would be going off with Konrad to her mother's to be bored over coffee and cake, as she was every Sunday.

Victor the dog, who was so homely that other dogs in the park ran away when he wanted to play with them, barked; a moment later I heard Robert's key in the door. "Woo-hoo!" I thought. "Company!"

But I rejoiced too soon. Robert had brought work home with him, which happened now and then, and couldn't be disturbed.

The last time he did this, I tried to bring him to his senses but failed miserably. He hardly listened to me, said it was no concern of mine and that I was just jealous. He could do what he liked in his own apartment. And I couldn't do anything about it if I wanted to hang onto my room.

Robert was the head of a casting agency in West Hollywood that cast extras for commercials and music videos as well as TV and films. Allegedly he had cast at least 100 of the doomed passengers in *Titanic*, or at least this is the transparent story he told the clueless chicks who turned up in his office in equally transparent blouses and sometimes without underwear. Sometimes he took his "commission," as he called it, right there on the desk.

This particular Saturday night he brought one of his victims home with him again, some giggly little chick.

I stayed in my room and turned the music up.

I could still hear the giggling. Apparently they had stayed in the living room, and presumably were on the couch, which was on the other side of the wall of my room (and Americans love building thin walls out of wood).

I turned the music up even louder.

No more giggling was heard; instead, the pop of a cork from a champagne bottle and then shortly after the sound of two glasses clinking as they toasted the almost-for-sure role in the almost-for-sure sequel to *Miss Congeniality*. And then more giggling.

My door opened. The dog, the fur of whose fore-forefathers was used to make winter caps that made defenseless children miserable, came into my room and wagged its tail.

"I know you're going to hate me," I said, "but could we please go for a walk? Just a half an hour, till the two of them have finished."

I took pity on myself. The sun had gone down long ago, and nobody would see us together.

I meet James in the park; he's suddenly standing in front of me.

I pull him behind a bush and shoo Victor away.

We talk to each other.

It's dark and I can hardly see.

James coddles me. He kisses my neck, strokes my chest, my stomach, and unbuttons my pants.

I pull his T-shirt over his head and toss it away. It gets caught in the branches of a tree. Then I hold his head steady and dig my fingers into the back of his neck, which he really likes. I hear him moan softly.

Now James gets up and takes his pants off. I feel his warm hands on my hips. He slowly turns me around and presses his hot body against mine.

And that's when the telephone rings.

It didn't really ring, but I could hear it clearly, and James took off.

It was enough to make you pull out your pubic hair: I couldn't even have sex mentally with James anymore.

My imagination no longer obeyed me and was organizing its own parties in my head (perhaps it had fallen victim to yellow fever and didn't know it yet?).

Something always happened to destroy the tension: either I threw out my back or Victor came running in and started watching; sometimes it started to rain, or James suddenly turned into Adam, who looked at me, shaking his head, and asked about the hand brake.

Frustrated, I lay my hand on the blanket and closed my eyes, but I couldn't fall asleep. So I counted men again.

CHAPTER 11

Never trust a guy who wears out five different sex partners in one week, above all:
—if one is more unspeakable than the other
—if the week in question is only Wednesday to Sunday, and
—if he'll only own up to half of them afterwards

A couple of miles down the street from my apartment was a kindergarten. I always drove past it on my way home. From the outside it looked a tad shabby. The red paint was peeling off the walls; hanging in the windows were sun-bleached art projects curled at the edges.

Whether there were actually children there, I didn't know, because I left the house well after noon and seldom came home before sundown.

There was always a large piece of paper hanging on the door to the school on which was written the "Letter of the Week." When I moved in with Robert, it was "T" as in triumph, twitchy, trumpet and ta-da!

Every Monday the letter was changed, moving along the alphabet.

Now it was up to "D" as in depression.

The number of my friends—this means the people who used to come to my parties to break my expensive champagne glasses or to puke in my sink because they never made it to the toilet—had significantly dropped off. On some days the inbox for my e-mail was completely empty: not even Heiko, an old friend from volunteer days, who would send me the current weather report from Hamburg with the subject line "I envy you, you bum!"

My depression increased in inverse proportion, as per the saying, "Be miserable and prosper." Which was particularly excruciating, here in the land of cheerful supermarket clerks ("Hi! How're you today?"), since frequent exposure to the sun cranks up the production of the happiness hormone, the psyche is saying, "Leave me alone! It's no good for me!" And who was the one who had to endure the squabbling between the two?

Right.

I looked at the world through sunglasses with dark gray lenses. It was as if I were driving 15 instead of 30 on a street where you could go 25. As if I were standing on a dance floor and could no longer remember the steps.

You never really wake up, the corners of your mouth lock when you attempt to lift them, and you can't even cheer yourself up with the very silliest 80s songs, because even their very silliness gets on your nerves and you wonder at the arrogance of someone trilling "I should be so lucky lucky lucky lucky."

Also not helpful: I couldn't find my Carpenters CD, it was gone. Untraceable.

It was awful.

And there were also certainly glimmers of light. Every day I felt more and more American. I had learned that when you're shopping you don't just grab the first bread that outwardly resembles a German whole-grain bread. How often I had wondered at the strange taste of my tuna fish sandwich until I finally looked at the package and saw that this "healthy, multi-grain" bread I had grabbed was sweetened with honey or brown sugar—or both!

When someone calls trying to sell me insurance or some particularly cheap phone plan, I hang up immediately because I learned that it's usually just a recorded message anyway and that I didn't have to come up with polite excuses.

"I'm sorry, this is a bad time. I'm just filling my pool."

I had also reduced my number of tickets for not-entirely-by-the-book parking from two a week down to one a month (who knew that those prettily painted curbs actually meant things like, say, a loading zone?). And when I drove into a parking garage in Santa Monica, I not only noted what level I had parked on, but I also paid attention on the way back so I actually went into the right parking garage, since they'd built a bunch right next to each and they all looked exactly the same, which was totally confusing, and they were only differentiated one from the other by the numbers 1 through 4, which of course I never noticed when I first drove in.

I spent one whole afternoon in Number 3, running frantically back and forth from the first to the eighth level calling out to Matlock, looking for him (I was supposed to meet Gavin and was already a half an hour late); until finally the police drove me over to Number 1, and told me as I got out of the car that, by the way, the number of the garage is on the ticket. So have a good day.

And when, strolling along Melrose Avenue, I was followed by Fatty Baldwin again, I remained cool and didn't get annoyed that I didn't have my camera along.

But all these small successes couldn't distract me from the fact that I hadn't seen or heard a thing of James. Whenever I called him, he wasn't home. Or he wasn't picking up. He also never called back. That could be because I didn't leave a message, at least not the usual kind. But who else would not say anything for half a minute, just breathing on the recording, not leaving his name? Who but me?

I spent a whole week doing that, sitting at home and waiting. Calling; breathing; hanging up. Getting annoyed; redialing; hanging up again.

I also dialed Adam's number once, but only once. Or maybe twice (the third time didn't count because the line was busy).

After the fourth time I decided to distract myself with some physical training. If was soon to die alone and forsaken, at least it wasn't going to without running wild a bit first. After all, I was in my early 30s, and had to make the most of it.

On Gay Pride Weekend I met a perfectly acceptable, if also chinless, guy whose throat began directly beneath his upper lip. But that didn't bother me. I had my own chin. Every Friday night he sat in a two-square-foot cubbyhole at Ultra Suede hanging jackets and coats on hangers.

"That'll be two dollars. Thank you! Have fun!"

When I, as the last customer, picked up my jacket, I picked him up as well. I was drunk; I had seen Adam (officially, of course, I hadn't seen him, just as little as he saw me).

We weren't even all the way into his apartment yet when he lay without a chin and without his pants on the kitchen table and stretched his legs in the air.

I poked around in him a bit, like a little kid who you set a bowl of spinach in front of when he'd much rather have had something else.

For some reason I gave him my telephone number, and the next three days he was chewing my different-sized ears off with when-were-we-going-to-see-each-other-again, so that I finally told him I had a boyfriend for whom I had especially left Germany.

I also gave this story the following evening to the Mexican police officer who had a pelvis on him as if he gave birth to twins several times a day. Breached. He was recently divorced, but wasn't off on relationships as long as no one wanted one with him.

He bought me a couple of drinks. I showed my gratitude in the bathroom.

"Man oh man!" he whispered as he disgustedly pulled a crinkly hair out of his mouth. "If you were my boyfriend, you'd have to shave yourself down there. And who knows, maybe it'd make your dick look bigger."

Unfortunately I was too drunk that evening to tell him where he could stick his beauty tips, and that I could help myself to a razor anytime, while only advanced plastic surgery could take on that killer pelvis of his.

It didn't go any better with the computer programmer from Silver Lake (the neighborhood next to Los Feliz) and his waterbed. We met at Akbar, a locale for alternative types who smoked inside despite the ban and therefore came off as incredibly bohemian and European (but what does that mean in a country where you can't smoke inside or drink alcohol outside?).

"Hey, you must be from Germany," he said before I had hardly finished saying my first sentence.

"Hallogutentagwiegehtsaufwiedersehendiesistmeineblauesauto!"

I could forgive him his execrable high school German, but not that later on he tried for half an hour to turn me over onto my stomach on the waterbed, while I much prefer a stable side position, and kept rolling back over until I finally got fed up and staggered back home.

After all this I was ready to enter a little cloister in the mountains for the rest of my life or to marry a charming young woman. After all, I was in my early 30s, and had to make the most of it.

I practiced abstinence. No more sex; no alcohol.

I felt strong and, above all, well rested. My body could use the time off I had given it to relax; it wasn't losing precious time anymore breaking down martinis and red wine.

A life without men and drinks, for a week.

And what's the big deal with that? I already endured it once for 16 years (right at the beginning) and it wasn't such a bad time.

The suggestion came from a strange man.

"I know it's hard because the weekend begins tonight. That's the reason I hate having to tell someone this on a Friday. But otherwise the effect of the penicillin is lost immediately. So: No sex and no alcohol for the next seven days"

The doctor at the health clinic smiled at me, almost apologetically, and sent me out to the receptionist. I was supposed to set up an appointment with her to come back in two weeks to pick up my test results.

By that time hopefully it wouldn't burn like a bitch anymore when I peed.

"My god, a victim of the yellow fever!" Gavin screamed when I called him.

"That's not funny, Gavin," I said.

Then he gave me the address of this clinic.

The way to the exit was through the waiting room; four young men were sitting there and a pregnant woman, on her lap a small child leafing listlessly through a brochure on the early detection of breast cancer in women. Everyone had a fixed point at which they silently stared, on the ceiling or the floor; the natural stream of Californian twaddle was neutralized within these walls.

They made me sad, all of them, and I wished I could drive their fears away, maybe with a diagnosis of an inflamed bladder or an innocuous penicillin-treatable case of the clap ("no sex and no alcohol for a week"). I wished I could spare them the worst.

"Well? Meet anyone new lately?" Paula wanted to know when she called me.

"No, nobody."

In my mind's eye I saw the Mexican police officer leaning against the toilet; he buttoned his pants up. I considered him quite likely to be an arsonist.

Turns out I was right.

"Okay, just tell me about the ones who were nice."

Paula knew me too well.

"You don't wanna hear it, Paula. Really. And believe me, I also don't want to tell it."

"Okay, fine."

I would have preferred that we had ended the conversation there.

"Then I'll tell you something. This weekend I ran into Daniel. My god, how many years were you two together? He didn't look good. Maybe thinner than before or something, I'm not sure. Are you two still in touch?"

"Sometimes. But it's been a while. Did you talk?"

"No, I was out with the girls, and saw him sitting at the bar. By the time I tried to get over to him, he was already gone."

Before talking with Paula, I felt like a marathon runner whose body hasn't been producing serotonin for about umpteen miles, and who suddenly notices that he's taken a wrong turn somewhere and can't see anyone around for far and wide. He's horrifically tired and just wants to fall over.

After I hung up, I began to fall over.

The telephone rang, but I just couldn't pick up.

Somewhere an answering machine clicked on.

"Hi, this is Aaron. This is a message for Ben. Hey listen, next week I have to go to San Diego to a convention. Maybe I could drop by over the weekend. Do you have time? Call me. Take care."

On one of those nights I would prefer not to remember (and in far less detail), and about which I wouldn't tell Paula, I lost my wallet.

One morning I was standing in Starbucks ordering my coffee, and it was gone.

I stood there not only tired and hungover, but also fairly addle-brained, since how was I supposed to wake up properly without my morning coffee? Besides, it would take forever before I would get my passport, my credit card, and another naked photo of Paula.

The first problem solved itself, since the shock jump-started my circulation; and then they gave me a latte on the house because I was such a regular and charming customer.

Everything else would take a couple days, the woman at the hotline said when I cancelled my credit card.

At the club, which I barely remembered being at, they couldn't find anything. I got the same answer from the taxi company whose cab had brought me home at three in the morning.

And when, a few days before, I had assumed that just about nothing could make my mood worse—this was all I needed.

So I was all the more happy about Aaron's call.

We had a shared a room back in the day at the university in Utah.

He was studying finance and marketing, but was himself always broke because he could never figure out how long he had to wait till the next check would come from his parents.

On a regular basis, at the middle of the month, sometimes earlier, he'd hit me up for a few dollars.

"Don't you think you should study something simple, Aaron, like consumer studies?" I sometimes suggested to him.

"The trick," he said, "isn't to have money yourself, but to know who you can get it from. You also don't know what Hamlet says to Ophelia in the fifth act, but you know where to look it up."

I always thought this comparison didn't work, especially since Ophelia drowns in the fourth act.

We threw wild parties in our room. Aaron was dealing in cigarettes and vodka at the time, and kept the stock in his closet. It was like paradise.

He got busted in his third year, by which time I was already back in Germany trying to give up smoking.

One of the students blew the whistle on him when he didn't want to sleep with her. At that time, Aaron didn't sleep with any woman twice.

Oddly enough, he didn't have to leave the university. Aaron never wanted to tell me how he had pulled that off.

Later he married the university president's daughter, and moved to Houston.

I would love to have known what kind of convention he was attending in San Diego. We hadn't seen each other in two years. At that time Aaron was already divorced.

His visit would be a welcome change. I shot him a quick e-mail, and arranged for someone to cover for me at the theater over the weekend.

On Thursday Aaron cancelled his visit.

On Friday evening suddenly Scott and Pete were standing at my door, and said I had just five minutes to pack a few things for the weekend.

They wouldn't tell me the destination of the trip.

"You'd just hunker down in the house in a bad mood. You can do that again next weekend."

Scott greeted me with a kiss, as usual with a slightly open mouth, and dropped into an armchair.

"And where am I supposed to have a bad attitude this weekend without money and a without a credit card if I don't have it here?" I asked.

"Don't ask so many questions, just pack! Otherwise we'll never get out of here today."

He took the remote and turned on the TV. There was a show on the Discovery Channel about mummies in Southern Peru.

Pete plopped onto Scott's lap and blocked his view.

As he ran his hands over his boyfriend's freshly shaved head, he looked at me.

"Let yourself be surprised, hon. Just be sure to bring a warm sweater along. You know, it's always a little cool in San—uh—San—shit!"

Scott gave Pete a clout on the head and shoved him off his lap.

"Okay, can we get going? In a little bit I'm not going to feel like it anymore."

I halfheartedly threw some clothes together (at any rate, I came across my Carpenters CD; it was in my backpack the whole time), and heard Pete in the background yammering that he was sorry, but it was well known that he couldn't keep a secret.

Scott only said that he was astoundingly good at it during his last affair with that waiter.

And so I considered briefly whether I might not tend my depression better at home, but next thing I knew we were driving north on the 405 and DJ Pete was featuring his Madonna collection.

I hated San Francisco.

Pete's sister Jody had let us use her apartment; this weekend she was at an important women's demonstration up in Sacramento. I wondered what connection the siblings might have. The one was into women, the other men; the one listened to Melissa Etheridge and Tracy Chapman, the other would only consider participating in a demonstration on the condition that it was carried live on TV (and then he'd wear his Material Girl T-shirt).

"Why is she hitting the street this time? To demand fashionable haircuts for long-haired lesbians?"

Scott was squatting by Jody's refrigerator looking at photos held to it by hamburger- and hot dog-shaped magnets.

"Can we go now?"

Pete made a face and ran his hand over his thin hair. He complained about having a headache because Scott had hit him. The clout he had given him the night before was allegedly to blame.

Scott replied that the headache was Pete's own fault because he was always having his hair dyed, which really only meant that he still had hair.

"But not for long!" With this Scott seemed to have won the fight. Pete's hair was at any rate getting thinner and thinner because he was always rubbing this stuff into it.

"Don't be jealous. At least I still have hair to rub stuff into."

Scott didn't answer. It was clear that his boyfriend saw it as the fate of his hair to be dyed every ten days.

Pete stood in the open apartment door and rattled the keys impatiently.

We were staying in the middle of the Castro, on a street parallel to Castro Street, somewhat up the hill, and you couldn't go out the door without stumbling over guys who were making out or hand-holding lesbian couples. It was living hell.

And, despite the sunshine, it was cold; a cool wind pushed through the streets.

We started the day with a late breakfast and premature martinis (it was okay for me again, the seven days were nearly over) in a small café on a side street.

Scott regretted that we had slept so late. He described what early morning was like in San Francisco, with the fog creeping through the streets and up into the hills.

"The best backdrop for English whodunits," he gushed. "Sometimes it's like that all the way into the afternoon. Then the Golden Gate Bridge is completely hidden."

Pete had his nose stuck in some fifth-rate tabloid; he was inhaling current Madonna news from four months ago and filling us in.

"What? She won't sing 'Vogue' anymore? Then I won't go to her concerts!"

Scott observed the wizened olive in his glass for a moment and said:

"You know, sometimes I wonder whether I should have him put to sleep. On the other hand, you've never seen anyone who can give such terrific car head like he can. It's not an easy position to be in. What should I do?"

He put his arm around the somewhat resistant Pete and gave him a kiss that was eventually returned.

Thank you! My only friends in this city, in this country, on this continent, stabbed me in the back and were tormenting me with their dubious happiness.

I weighed two options in my mind: to call in Amnesty International or to run amok. I decided on a third possibility.

"Guys, I have to walk around a little. Now I have a headache, too. Let's meet back here in a couple hours."

I had no particular destination in mind other than outta there. And so I decided to approach San Francisco as I had other strange cities on earlier trips: I headed for the first intersection with a traffic light and went in the direction of the first green light I came upon. And went straight in that direction till I came to the next light.

It was a way of going about things that was as mindless as it was random, which was exactly why I loved it. (Daniel had called it "late-adolescent" as he rolled his eyes and tried in vain to fold up his idiotic map of the city.)

I went past blue and violet, mint green and pale yellow houses, a few of which had signs in the window: "For Rent: 3 rooms for $3,000. Pets okay." Sometimes people were sitting on the steps playing chess or listening to loud music and talking.

In between there were always bars, shops, or mini-flea-markets on the sidewalk where you could buy old books, glass vases or used shoes.

I began seeing fewer and fewer people, the number of traffic lights was also decreasing, and as the sun began to depart, I gradually got cold and decided to head back.

I very quickly got warm again when I realized that I had no idea in which direction I should go.

How long had I been pigheadedly going straight-on?

And was it possible that I had suddenly landed somewhere in a London suburb with Victorian houses?

Did this corner look familiar to me because I had walked past it or did it just look like a thousand other corners? And whose voice was that that just said "pardon me?" for the second time?

"Are you looking for something in particular? Maybe I can help you."

A friendly-looking, tall, blond man stood there in a leather coat and looked at me through his wire-rimmed glasses.

I was hoping he'd be able to tell me the way back to Jody's apartment in just a couple of sentences, but apparently mine was a more complicated case. Christopher—this was the man's name—wanted to walk along to show me.

Now, the likelihood of running into an actor, writer or a make-up artist on the streets of San Francisco was somewhat remote (in contrast to Los Angeles where a lot of gay guys describe their ideal partner as b: "not in the industry" right after a: "HIV-negative"). But Christopher worked as a freelance writer. He had even lived for a stretch in L.A. and had written for episodes 7,200 to 7,850 of *General Hospital*, but then moved back to his hometown, where his friends lived and no one called it "Frisco" or "SanFran."

Incidentally, the people of San Francisco traditionally have a love/hate relationship with the Los Angelinos, comparable to that which exists between people from Cologne and those from Dusseldorf (based, by the way, on similar superficial considerations).

I pictured Christopher in Los Angeles in an empty apartment surrounded by unpacked moving boxes, talking on the phone for hours with his friends. I felt sorry for him; I liked him.

"How do you endure it there?" he asked me. "I mean, it's not really a city. Huxley once said: Los Angeles is a hundred suburbs looking for a city. He was right."

We had arrived in front of the café where I was supposed to meet Scott and Pete. Music poured out onto the street along with a loud mishmash of voices. Not a trace of the two of them; I also didn't see them through the window.

How was I supposed to get home if I had missed them? How was I supposed to pay for a train or plane ticket without a credit card?

It was seven at night, almost dark. I was half an hour too late.

"I wouldn't really call it endurance. By the way, we're here. Thanks so much for saving me."

I put out my hand to him, but he ignored it.

"What brought you to the City of Angels anyway?"

"That's a pretty long story. At any rate, thanks again."

I opened the door and set my foot on the threshold.

"Are your friends there?" Christopher asked.

"No, but they should be here any minute."

"I'd really like to have a drink with you," he said, and held the door open so he could gently nudge me in.

I felt like I was losing control, and didn't trust myself to look at him.

We sat at a table by the window. Christopher laid his coat on the chair between us and smiled at me.

"So tell me the story. Then maybe I'll understand why you're so uptight. But let me get our drinks first."

I woke up to a warm, wet tongue licking my feet. It was dark in the room, and for a second I thought I was at Scott's and that the wet tongue belonged to Siegfried or Roy.

I thought I recognized something that looked like a dog.

I must not have noticed it yesterday. Or was Jody back early from her demonstration?

I had to laugh when I thought of the haircut joke Scott made yesterday, when he hardly had any hair himself. (Adam always called lesbian parties "bad hair days.")

I noticed when I laughed that my head wasn't doing real well with being shaken like that. Still chuckling, I lay back carefully and massaged my temples.

"What's so funny?" a voice next to me asked.

A mild earthquake, roughly the strength of the ones that plague the San Francisco Bay area on a regular basis, rocked my skull as I turned my head to the side a tad too fast.

"Take cover under a solid table (a desk, for example) or within a doorframe" shot for a second through my aching head.

Christopher grinned at me.

"What're you doing here?" I asked and rubbed my brow as I moved over to the edge of the bed.

"Very charming, really. I'll go get you some aspirin."

Still grinning, he climbed out of bed and disappeared into the semidarkness. Though I could still tell he was naked.

Hopefully Scott and Pete were still sleeping. What I was really not in the mood for was their dumb questions and their even dumber commentary on the way home. ("Honey!" Pete would say. "Yesterday Adam, James today, and tomorrow Christopher! I assume he's got a boyfriend, right?")

Christopher came back and handed me a glass of water and a couple of aspirin. Then he went to the window and opened the curtains.

Glaring daylight admonished me to never drink alcohol again.

From between my fingers, which I had held up in front of my eyes as a shield from the light, I could make out the delectable details of his body: a respectable share of muscle (not too much), hair (not too little), and a high-voltage-symbol tattoo (not too big) in the small of his back. It reminded me a little of the lightning on the weather map on the TV news.

I washed the pills down as Christopher climbed back into bed. He looked at me, his head propped on his arm.

"Did you run into the others?" I asked.

"No."

He slid his hand onto my stomach and began fondling me.

"How late is it, then? Hopefully they haven't left already."

With that, I jumped out of bed and grabbed my briefs.

Christopher sat up with a sigh and watched me.

"I imagine you're going to have to see about that in the other apartment. Here it's just me and Fluffy."

As if on cue, the dog got up and thereby freed my pants and left shoe, which he'd been lying on, and ran to the bed, his tail wagging.

So I wasn't at Pete's sister's.

"It's a shame you've got to go already. It was really nice last night."

"Yeah," I replied, without having even an approximate idea as to what happened.

I was holding my jacket in my hand and just wanted to get out of the apartment.

"Just one question."

Now of course he was going to want my telephone number. Or to know whether I had a boyfriend. Or when we would see each other again.

I slowly pulled my jacket on and looked at him suspiciously.

"Who taught you all that?"

Christopher grinned at me.

Holy shit! What did I do? The splits? Acrobatics? Bondage games? Hopefully nothing that involved Fluffy. And could dogs get the clap? (How horrible! They wouldn't do anything else all day but run around the neighborhood pissing.)

I took my jacket off again and sat warily next to Scott on the bed.

"What exactly do you mean?

"Well, where should I begin ... I'm not sure if I'm up on all the technical terms."

"That's okay."

Half my life flashed before my eyes, above all the last few days and nights. Nobody had complained; on the other hand, I certainly wasn't the David Copperfield of casual sex. From that moment I would never drink alcohol again.

Christopher put his hand on the nape of my neck and looked at me.

"Relax! I just wanted to give you a little scare. Nothing happened at all. You also probably weren't capable of anything. Everything's on the up and up. I don't take advantage of such situations. And that wasn't particularly easy. You were snuggling up to me so sweetly."

San Francisco experienced its second great earthquake that morning, and even if no one except me noticed: The impact with which the stone fell from my heart, if someone had measured it, would have registered 8.3 on the Richter Scale.

Before I left Christopher's apartment, I asked for his telephone number and promised to come back again to San Francisco soon.

It was a beautiful day; I had no desire to leave. The streets were swarming with people; happy couples went about the neighborhood hand-in-hand, their broad smiles infectious.

Christopher had told me exactly how to get to Jody's. There I ran into two guys making out in the doorway, who laughingly formed an honor guard to let me through.

I clapped them on the shoulder and wished them all the best and a good day.

CHAPTER 12

You should take a much more demanding look at your guy early on, since:
—once the two of you are really into it, it's usually too late
—murder is a capital offence in a lot of countries
—in the end, even Oprah can't do anything about it

The death that Robert should die is rather unspectacular.

It's not this slow slice with a utility knife followed by the removal of his bowels (which push out as soon as the abdominal wall is opened), which I stuff in his dumb mouth to keep him quiet if the long, gaping slit hasn't brought him to his senses. Then I can very slowly begin (he should have lost consciousness by now—the sooner the better) to cut his toes from his feet, one after the other, though I'd probably need a bone saw for that, maybe even an ax, certainly by the time I reached the ankle the task would be too much for a utility knife.

This would make lots and lots of freezer-ready portions, and for weeks, maybe months after the mysterious disappearance of his long-haired companion, Victor might suffer from grief but certainly not from hunger.

Then again, I've never really been able to stand that dog, so why am I being so considerate of him?

No, a hefty whack on the skull ought to suffice, the wine bottle on the table should do, and he'd slowly bleed to death with an especially long, sharp shard piercing his heart as he bid this world goodbye.

I confess that these hideous thoughts went through my head for a tenth of a second as I sat at home in the kitchen on that calamitous Sunday night.

We were very late getting back from San Francisco. I was dead tired and was looking forward to my bed.

Through the open kitchen door I could see Robert sitting at the table in front of a glass of wine, a corkscrew in his hand.

He was all smiles as I came into the kitchen. The dog, who couldn't be bothered to bark at possible intruders, began to yap and was sent into the living room. That was new.

"Good to see you. Have a good weekend?"

He got me a glass out of the cupboard, but I declined. I just wanted to sleep.

"Yeah, I lived there for a couple years, but it was too small for me, you know? And driving there is nuts, San Fran is nothing but one-way streets. And then the weather! Not me. Never again."

Robert was not to be stopped. Either he had a lonely weekend behind him with no private audiences with giggling models—or he wanted something from me.

"By the way, I have some good news for you, a couple things."

He looked at me expectantly. Apparently he wasn't ready to share the news with me until I tore my clothes off in a fit of enthusiasm and pounded my fists on the table.

"Maybe I could hear it?"

"Do you have anything planned tomorrow between one and four?"

Aha!

"It's no big deal. You wouldn't even have any lines," he said.

"Excuse me, Robert, but that's not the kind of good news I like getting on a Sunday night."

"It'll go really fast. Just a few minutes. You go there, you smile, they take your picture, and you're done. It can be very exciting."

If Robert was trying to turn me into a loser extra, he could totally forget it.

"Thanks, no. If I need excitement, I'll call my boss. But I'm certainly not going to a gathering of blond self-promoters."

He looked at me, pissed off. I was afraid that at any second he was going to call in the world's ugliest dog and sic it on me.

"Okay, that was obviously just the first part of the story. Then what?" I asked.

Robert's face relaxed instantly.

"It shoots at the end of the month. A family series about a funeral home in Los Angeles, and they're doing new episodes. From the makers of *American Beauty*, by the way. I wouldn't send you out to just any old bullshit."

I poured myself some of the wine.

"Great, and because you think I'd do such an uncannily good drowned corpse, I should go there tomorrow."

"I don't know exactly what they're looking for, but at the moment I don't have a lot of guys in their thirties on my list."

"Funny, I've got exactly the same problem," I said and sat down next to Robert at the table.

"So you'll do it? You know, it's just a casting thing. It doesn't matter if they don't take you."

"Which is my greatest hope, Robert."

"Cool, man! I'll write the address down for you later where you have to go tomorrow. Oh, right: if you can, dark clothes; a suit wouldn't be bad."

Robert got up and stood by the door.

"Oh, I almost forgot. There were two good-news things."

"I don't know if I can handle all the excitement, Robert."

"I'll grant you that."

"Okay fine, let's have it."

I had the corkscrew right in my hand (which wouldn't have been such a bad substitute for a knife) as Robert grinned at me.

"Your James called."

"Ohmygod, did someone die, hon?"

I wanted to ask Scott for help, but he wasn't home. Pete was too small. And too dramatic, as always.

"No, it's not like that. I need it for something else."

I knew Pete would die of excitement if I told him about the casting call. So I said some nonsense about a job interview, and that's why I needed the suit. I couldn't say anything more specific about it, it was all still real up in the air, etc.

Pete was appalled.

"Honey, you only wear a black suit to a funeral, you know, not to an interview like this. Sometimes I don't think you're really one of us. Where are your gay instincts? I just said that to Scott last night. No offense, but that green sweater you had on with those brown corduroys—oh my god!"

Scott didn't own a black suit. That's what I finally found out after ten minutes.

I couldn't reach Gavin, he was probably over at Ramon's, the guy who wanted to interview Nicole Kidman and the Pope. The two had been back together for a few days now (Gavin and Ramon, not Nicole and the Pope).

I left him a message asking to call me back as soon as possible about the suit.

I also spoke to the woman who had filled in for me when I was gone that weekend, a good-natured, slightly plump Texan with white hair: Mrs. Spring. She wore a gold chain around her neck, from which hung a pair of tinted glasses that were so gigantic they covered half her face when she put them on.

"It was enough to make you wanna tear your hair out! Saturday I barely sold half the tickets. That Tennessee Williams thing is still playing, with the crazy dog that gets shot in the end. No wonder nobody wants to see it."

I was glad she didn't blame me.

"Classic tragedy with a surprise outcome," I had said in the press release. "If you think you don't really cry anymore—this will convince you otherwise."

In one sense I was right: the desecration of a great American playwright, who couldn't defend himself, would be the only legitimate reason for many in our audience to cry (the review in the *Los Angeles Times* said something similar).

"Oh," Mrs. Spring continued, "and guess who was in the audience Saturday night: Kim Basinger. But she was there with a woman, not with her husband, that fat actor with all that hair on his chest. And just a little while ago on the TV they said the two of them were together again."

I was certain of it: If I had been working that evening, Alec Baldwin would have been there. We hadn't seen each other in a while; I almost missed him a little.

After that conversation, I tried in vain to reach Aaron. And I wanted to talk to Christopher to apologize for my idiotic behavior and to make sure I didn't have sex with him. I didn't want to be remembered as "the one who brought the clap to San Francisco." Unfortunately I couldn't find the piece of paper where I'd written his number.

End of the list. I had called every possible person I could think of just so I wouldn't be tempted to get in touch with James.

There was no way I wanted to call him, not now, not after he had disappeared into oblivion for over a month without a single reaction to my coded messages on his answering machine. He didn't need to think I'd been sitting around the house all these weeks waiting for some sign from him.

When the telephone rang, I was just emptying the dishwasher (Robert only unloaded it partially, depending on what he needed: a cup for his tea in the morning or two champagne glasses in the evening if he brought "work" home).

I jumped for the receiver. It was Paula.

"So should I call him or not?" I asked her.

"Do you want to see him again or not?"

One of her typical counter questions. I sometimes hated her for it.

"That's really not the point right now!"

I was waiting for her comeback, but she didn't say anything at all for a while.

"Speaking of seeing someone again, I accidentally ran into Daniel at the market. Then we went out for a coffee. And that lasted so long that I forgot to get home in time to drive Konrad to soccer practice … He's really deteriorated, Ben."

"Daniel?"

"He showed me these thick, weird-colored pills; he'd just come from the doctor."

"Shit."

It made me think of the pills I had to take over a week ago: one long, pale pink tablet and four little white ones. After two days, the burning was gone.

But the uncertainty remained. I still had to wait five days.

"I told him about you. He was very surprised to hear where you are now. He's still at his old apartment. Call him. I think he's very lonely."

And so, given current events, Paula cancelled the visit she'd announced for a couple weeks from now during Love Parade weekend.

This was incomprehensible to me, and not just because she missed me and I was looking forward to our reunion. How could someone, of her own free will, stay in Berlin on the worst weekend of the year, when hosts of unappealing people pour into the city?

Take a Saturday afternoon stroll around the ruins of the Memorial Church—that's enough to ruin your day.

You'll encounter at least one raver with a shaved chest and a gold loincloth who travelled from the province of Lower Saxony especially for this, so that he can belch wetly in your ear and kick his beer can into the gutter. You can't avoid the crewcutted techno fan in red knee-length sweatpants who's following you blowing a piercing whistle. Guaranteed you'll run into one of the numerous couples with blue-red dyed hair and matching glam outfits of 100% acrylic who are already so drunk by three in the afternoon that they're clinging to each other and can barely walk a straight line, forcing you to sidestep them into one of the ever-growing garbage heaps of beer cans and McDonald's bags, from which your nose picks up the pungent scent of a puddle of piss.

Nobody, of course, sees, hears, or smells this on TV.

No camera shows the heteros fucking in the Tiergarten along the shore of the canal (What's *that* about? Just because they don't have back rooms in their clubs, it's no reason to carry on like that!); and no local news reporter is interested in the howling women who went behind some hedge or other and accidentally piddled (every year, never enough port-a-potties) on their knee-high white mukluks.

Because Berlin environmentalists and arbiters of taste wanted to be finally rid of the Love Parade this year (or at least wanted to get the Tiergarten out of its clutches), Hannover, of all places, expressed interest in the belching, boozing and pissing ravers and their 300 tons of garbage, and somehow I supported the city in this with all my heart.

Apart from the horrific and horrifically important media pundits who speculated loudly in cafés as to whether they would bore themselves the night of the party watching it on TV or on Sony.

Well, the Love Parade stayed in Berlin—and so, in the end, did Paula.

I felt like I was going to my own funeral that afternoon as I drove in my white shirt and black pants to the casting call.

It was early July and so warm that the stick of lip balm lying in my car had turned into a puddle of lip balm. After an attempt to lubricate my lips, there was a hot, yellow clump hanging from my upper lip, just for a moment, until it dropped to my shirt, where it left a hideous spot.

So I had to go back to the apartment and change my shirt for the only other alternative, a black turtleneck sweater.

By now my enthusiasm level had dropped to below zero; still, I thought it was a good idea to go just to distract myself, though I was still really pissed at Robert.

It was a mistake.

I had to sit in some kind of waiting room. It was grotesque: Sitting there were a dozen people, all somewhere around my age, all in more or less somber attire or in suits, laughing and being loud and telling stories about other gigs as an extra.

"… and then he had to go past me really close and put his hand on my arm," a somewhat garishly made-up blonde in a pantsuit told her neighbor, who was wearing red sneakers with a black velvet dress.

"We'd done at least a hundred takes on the scene, and somewhere along the way he'd begun to press his arm against my breast. Just very lightly at first, but it became more and more apparent what he was up to, and I whispered to him: 'If you do that one more time, I'll kick you in the balls.' Then he left me alone."

"Really?" The woman in the red sneakers regarded her with awe. "I wouldn't have had the guts to do that."

I was accosted by a sweating, red-haired guy in a way-too-tight suit sitting next to me.

"Hey, weren't you also at that George Clooney shoot last month? The guy at the big gaming table—wasn't that you?"

"No, sorry," I said.

149

"I could've sworn … Oh well, never mind. By the way, I'm Danny."

He held out his hand.

Ever since grade school I've harbored an aversion to people who introduce themselves with just their first name or their y-ending nickname. This please-call-me-what-my-friends-call-me-so-you-can-be-my-friend-too-and-we-can-be-bored-together-over-a-Coke-someday stuff from Mikeys, Tommys and Bennys was so repellent to me that I still wondered sometimes why I ever exchanged another word with Daniel way back when.

"By the way, I'm Daniel. My friends call me Danny."

Daniel was a sweet guy, a surgeon, a few years older than me, and, in the eyes of a student, which I was at the time, incredibly attractive. He had a big apartment and a fast car; his refrigerator was always filled to capacity, while mine back home at my apartment share had for weeks only had a half slice of toast moldering away, already green with envy.

But most important of all: Daniel had so much hair on his chest you could have an Easter egg hunt in it.

When I nearly pushed him over in the subway New Year's morning—I was on my way home from a bad party; he was getting rolls for breakfast with his mother—he was 34 and had already been everywhere: South Africa, India, Israel, New Zealand.

"But I haven't been to paradise. Until today."

In hindsight it sounded kitschy; it sounded like Barbra Streisand songs at sunset, silk bed sheets and fancy champagne glasses on the nightstand, but when Daniel said it as I lay on his stomach after our first time having sex, running my sticky fingers through his thick chest hair, I thought I could easily tolerate a few years in this paradise.

It took me some time to find out that Daniel was a bore. In the end he became so boring that even his hair started falling out, which didn't look sexy at all—that type of boring.

I don't know anymore exactly what it was that first bothered me. Maybe the annual New Year's Day breakfasts at his mother's house, at which I regularly became ill because I drank too much coffee so I wouldn't fall back to sleep at 9:30 (!) in the morning (!); along with the accompanying admonishments from the hostess that too much coffee was bad for one's health (and of course her doctor son had to agree with her).

Or maybe rather it was Daniel's way of explaining the world to me. No matter whether we were somewhere on vacation or out shopping.

"Look at this, Ben, this food processor, everything it can do: squeeze fruit; knead dough; crush ice cubes, and here—with this you can even slice bread. You just put it in here and presto-change-o! You see?"

It was at the supermarket in front of the helpless clerk with big, thick-lensed glasses that I told Daniel I was going to move out. He was telling me for the fifteenth time the old story about how they always stocked certain chocolate candies and TicTacs at the check-out lines because of little kids waiting in the line when I told him I didn't love him anymore. Presto-change-o! Over! Done!

"Hey, what's the matter with you? You practicing for your big scene or what?

The red-haired guy withdrew his hand and regarded me with disgust as I wiped the tears from my face.

My name was called, and a small, friendly Asian woman took a picture of my swollen eyes.

CHAPTER 13

You shouldn't underestimate the advantages of life without a man,
—compared to life with a man for whom life with one man
   doesn't suffice
—compared to life with a woman who's already been with all of
   your buddies
—compared to life with a man who's a thousand times richer but
   also ten times older

You can get the most beautiful view of Los Angeles for just five dollars; that's how much a spot in the parking garage costs. It's a bit like the restaurant in the television tower in Berlin, except that here the whole thing isn't rotating and you can find your place when you come back from the bathroom.

You can see the valley, where the weekend traffic is cramming itself between the mountains; the Pacific; and down into the gigantic city, which, even on a clear day, you can't see to the end of.

Los Angeles, in contrast to New York and Berlin, is never hectic or stressful; even so, this spot in the Santa Monica mountains is like a peaceful oasis.

The air has the enchanting smell of fresh garlic that the Tulbaghia violacea shrubs give off, whose non-Latin names include both "society garlic" and "forest lily" and are valued by Latinos and non-Latinos alike because they keep away mosquitoes.

With their pink blooms they're one of many specks of color from the various types of plants growing in the garden of the J. Paul Getty Museum.

With its antique sculptures and furniture, major European painters and modern photographers, it's the richest and greatest museum in the world—so rich (I know this from Adam) that the Getty staff has to spend half a million dollars a day because the vast capital in the private endowment brings in so much interest. This Getty guy is definitely marrying material—if only he weren't so dead.

This garden, high above the city, is the best and prettiest place for reflection. But today I couldn't get my head clear. The garlic smell prompted images of Adam … He was standing in the kitchen in front of a steaming pot and called to me that I should be so kind as to not cut the mushrooms so small and wondered whether he might be able to count on them today. I continued cutting extra slowly and began to whistle a Carpenters song, which, I knew from experience, made him mad.

Now he stopped cooking.

Without a word, Adam took the knife out of my hand and pushed me aside so he could cut the mushrooms himself. He never even mentioned that I had cut the last pieces into teeny little hearts. He threw them silently onto the plate with the other mushrooms.

I stuck my finger into a pot of cream standing next to the plate and wiped it on Adam's neck.

He didn't react.

I stuck the next finger with cream into his right ear and turned it around a few times back and forth.

Adam stopped briefly, but then continued working unperturbed.

Now I went a few steps around him and also filled his left ear.

He laid the knife slowly on the table, grabbed the pot of cream, and held it over my head.

"You won't do it," I said.

He gave me this boyish grin.

"Who's going to stop me?"

First I felt a tiny drop on my brow, then he poured the entire thing over my head. I tried to reach for Adam with my eyes shut. Finally I wiped them till I could see again, and saw him standing over by his pot again as if nothing had happened.

My sticky hands stamped a first-class imprint on the back of his dark blue shirt.

"You didn't do that," he said slowly.

"I'm afraid that unfortunately you're going to have to take off your shirt."

To this day I don't know how Adam got the bag of flour so quickly that he dumped in my face, upon which occurred what to an outside observer would have looked like a fight. In actuality we were trying to tear each other's clothes from our bodies, and to bring the mess on the kitchen floor to perfection with a couple spritzes of our own.

Nobody talked about mushrooms anymore that night.

The sun began to go down. In the distance I could make out Adam's building; strictly speaking, I saw a couple blocks the size of half a mushroom.

I decided to call him. His birthday was in a few days.

Maybe he was home; maybe he was cooking something delicious right now—maybe an apple pie for the guy with the teeth-for-two.

On the railway that brought me back down to my car, I changed my mind. Instead I'd call Scott. Pete had just flown off around the world again; I'd have him all to myself.

The Abbey hadn't seen me in a while. I couldn't shake the feeling that someone was watching me there. It wasn't the usual gay gaping you run into when you have funny ears or you had sex the night before and are still beaming like Geena Davis after a night with Lorenzo

Lamas. It was as if someone there—someone specific; always the same person—had me in his sights. His eyes drank my beer, they read my lips, and sometimes they wanted to know the color of my underwear. And I couldn't figure out who it was.

I felt safe with Scott. I even hoped his hello kiss would be more intense than usual (the end justifies the tongue) to get rid of my stalker once and for all.

All the tables were taken.

We ordered something to eat, and I went to the bathroom while Scott waited at the bar and had our drinks made.

When I got back—and I'm not one of those people who have to try out every scent in the bathroom, nor do I have to sit when I pee, but I always wash my hands afterwards (this isn't a given even among gayboys), during which I wondered how I could tell Scott I was thinking about calling Adam without him thinking I was having a relapse; so let's say: away about three minutes—I found Scott deep in conversation with some cute young guy, who was introduced to me as Jackson or Jason. One of these wusses who drinks his margaritas without salt.

I mumbled my polite nice-to-meet-you and hoped he'd soon piss off. But instead Scott invited him to sit with us when I spotted a table freeing up.

Jason/Jackson worked as a film set decorator, was in his mid-twenties, and had just moved to Los Angeles. Information that was, so it seemed, as new to Scott at this moment as it was to me, and it wasn't quite clear here who had picked up whom. But it became apparent relatively quickly that Scott was aiming for a more intimate togetherness during the course of the evening, and that the lucky winner wasn't named Ben and certainly not Pete.

I'd never seen Scott use a napkin so much. After every bite he wiped under his mustache so that not the merest embarrassing crumb of his meal remained.

Jason/Jackson stroked the hair behind his ears with every dumb sentence he said (and truth be told, except for dumb sentences he didn't seem to have much going on, but Scott would find that out later), which made his shoulders shrug a little.

I bid them good night as I was still swallowing my last bite. As I was going, I thought I heard something like "We can't go by me." But it could just as well have been something equally deep as "You can't buy me" or "You can boff me."

At any rate, Paula agreed when she called the next day, and said that it was really a gross injustice that someone with a steady boyfriend would even think of starting something up with another man (or, alternatively, another woman) instead of getting down on his knees and paying homage to his beloved every day, kissing his feet in gratitude and devotion, when there are people—she added—who feel so lonely that they don't know which of their ex-boyfriends they miss the most.

I chose not to pick up on her reference, and came directly to the actual subject at hand.

"I'm just not sure if my calling Adam is a good idea."

"Excuse me, but certainly you mean James."

"No," I said.

"Are you sure you know what you want?"

"No."

"Forget it! Happy endings exist only in Hollywood, Ben."

I didn't say anything.

"I still have the letter from Adam that he sent a couple weeks ago. Do you want to read it now?"

"No."

"I'll send it to you if you want."

"But I don't want it, Paula."

I had just hung up when the fax machine started to print something out. I folded Adam's letter in two, and then tore it in two right down the middle and threw the pieces in the garbage.

A tiny ping announced the next fax.

> "You can throw it away as often as you like. I'm sending you the
> letter once a day until you finally do something!
> Yours always, P."

How many individual pieces do you get when you fold a piece of paper two times down the middle and then tear it in two two times down the middle?

   a) 8 equal-sized pieces
   b) 9 different-sized pieces
   c) 12 different-sized pieces
      or
   d) 16 equal-sized pieces

Surprisingly enough, answer b is correct. You get one big piece, four little ones (which all together make one big one), and another four average-sized longish pieces, each of which is about as big as two of the little ones.

I couldn't figure out any mathematical formula that would explain this phenomenon, but that also wasn't what I had in mind as I retrieved the pieces of Adam's letter from the wastebasket and began putting it back together.

> "Dear Ben,
> Hopefully you arrived safely in Germany.
> I can't tell you how sorry I am about everything.
> I don't know what was going on with me, and I don't know what's

going on with me now when I write to say that I miss you, little
guy.
I can't wait to hear from you, and I hope you won't hang up if
I call you.
Adam"

This letter was sheer impudence. And telltale! Three of the four sentences began with "I." Adam was only thinking of himself.

If his letter had, till now, consisted of nine pieces, after being read
it became even more indecipherable. In the end the individual pieces were so small that doing anything more to it (and counting the
results) would require the hands of Chinese child laborers.

I flushed the whole thing down the toilet.

As if intoxicated by the idea of being free of Adam, I wanted to
put even more things in order. I began sorting through newspapers
that I had carelessly thrown under the bed or onto the cabinet once
I had cannibalized them for my column. At first there were three
piles: one for *Entertainment Weekly*, one for the *Enquirer*, and even
People Magazine got its own heap. Then I wavered between two possible internal organizing principles: Should I sort issues by alphabetical order according to the star on the cover or chronologically
by publishing date?

I decided on the second option (Julia Roberts and Nicole Kidman
had so many cover stories that I'd have had to do a special file for
them anyway), and by the end of the evening I was a happy man.

Contented, I picked up the phone. The other end of the line was
quiet for a moment, then: "Nice of you to call. To tell the truth ...
I'm a bit surprised."

It was good to hear his voice. I remembered how it sounded when
I'd have my head on his chest and could hear his voice vibrating in
every pore.

"I'm surprised myself that I even called you."

That wasn't entirely true. I had planned it while I was at the clinic that morning waiting for the results of my test.

"Yeah, that doesn't surprise me at all. So how've you been the past few weeks?" he asked.

"Fantastic. Couldn't be better."

Of course that only described my immediate emotional state, the liberating close of two long, excruciating weeks, in which I, in my mind, picked up weird-colored pills from the pharmacy accompanied by a bone-thin Daniel; sometimes, right before falling asleep, I'd see Paula sitting in a black veil beside my bed, and she'd be trying to give me some lemon juice (minus martini) with a feeding cup; earlier she had changed my diaper for the second time in just a few hours because I could no longer control my bowels.

I had now learned these fears were unnecessary. My little souvenir from the police officer was all healed (the doctor liked calling it "the clap"; I didn't care as long as I was rid of it—after all, you don't name a miscarriage—not after the fact, at any rate), and my HIV test came out negative.

"A provisional all-clear," the doctor whispered to me kill-joyfully.

I had adjusted the number of my encounters with divorced Mexicans and chinless coat check boys down to two (what did he care about the number of my sexual indignities when I was feeling like I had liquid barbed wire flowing through my loins?).

"You should be tested again in two, three months, to be totally sure."

But at the moment I didn't really want to know about that.

So instead I talked about the newspaper, and that I hadn't heard from Carstensen for a few weeks, from which I presumed that either he or my column was dying and he didn't have the heart to tell me, and that presumably he had written those readers' letters himself to keep my confidence up.

He also hadn't said a thing about my monothematic tract on Julia Roberts, including my prophecy that next she'd start going after cameramen, since after Benjamin Brett there was hardly a single actor left in Hollywood whom she hadn't broken up with, broken an engagement to, or divorced.

I also casually mentioned my weekend in San Francisco and the nice men there.

No reaction.

I told him about Christopher, how I met him, and that he wanted to visit me soon.

No comment.

I was about to give up when he finally asked:

"Could we make another date? At the Abbey maybe?"

James could be so nice, when he finally did what you expected him to do.

CHAPTER 14

Keep away from men who bite their nails
—even if it's only their own nails
—even if it's only the fingernails
—even if they can bring Adam back to you

The first row of seats was nearly empty. On the left side of the aisle sat a somewhat heavyset young man with his arm around a woman wearing a skin-colored dress with lace trim through which everything was visible. She was barely twenty, but her eyes looked old and sad. Not because of the deceased, but because of the drugs with which she primarily sustained herself.

The coffin stood in the background, on it a large and expensive-looking wreath of lilies. Next to it was a cascade of even more expensive bouquets and still more wreaths.

I was standing in a group of two men and two women near the entrance to some manner of chapel where the funeral service was coming to an end, and was holding a glass in my hand. In it was something that looked like champagne, but I wasn't allowed to drink a drop of it. Every now and then a girl in an apron came around and poured a little of the fake champagne into a pail she carried around with her.

We were forbidden to speak with our fellow mourners, not even whispering. But we had to move our lips and act as if we were animatedly chatting with one another.

"Rolling!" someone yelled, then someone else did too, and finally it was quiet and the scene could begin.

A pale young guy with a round face and red hair was talking with one of the mourners, a very elegant woman around fifty. She looked a little like Brenda, Adam's girlfriend, with the exception that this woman was an actress and could carry herself confidently in a pair of high heels. The guy was one of the owners of the funeral parlor, and he was trying somewhat ineptly to comfort the sobbing woman while he seemed to be looking for something in his sports coat.

"Stop! Cut! Shit!" someone yelled, and the man who must have been the director, since he was the only person besides the actors who had his own chair, chewed out this woman who had come running out in a panic from behind a wall. In her hand she had a white Kleenex which she stuck in the funeral director's breast pocket. A man around fifty wearing glasses with half-lenses popped up next to her and began powdering both actors' foreheads. The red-haired guy looked over at me just for a second just as I was whispering to my dialogue partner about how bored I was, and then took his position again.

Finally they started again.

I held that glass in my hand for hours, and the more it was emptied, the thirstier I became.

I cursed Robert in my mind, and noticed that I was also hungry. Only two short scenes had been shot. I softly asked my partner in the hideous black sack dress, who held so strictly to the no-talking rule that she nearly dislocated her jaw, when the next break might be. She just shook her head and continued making exaggerated lip movements as if she were about to devour me.

After an hour someone called a break. The girl with the apron came and took our glasses away and put them on a tray. The red-haired guy with the round face undid the top button on his shirt and was led, laughing loudly, up a flight of stairs by a young woman in a baseball cap with a folder under her arm.

We extras had our own place in the garden, where there was a tent with coffee and cold drinks but nothing to eat. So that we wouldn't get our clothes messy, it was said.

The crew was huge. Other than the extras, there were at least 30 to 40 other people running around carrying either walkie-talkies, clipboards, or water bottles whose job description you could never quite figure out.

The woman with the big mouth chattered at me excitedly the entire time (now that she was finally allowed), and told me how much she loved this series, how happy she was to be able to be on it, and that the woman with long red-blond hair who had just come out of the house to have a cigarette was the conservative and clueless mother of the family and that the red-haired moon-faced guy was one of her children and, by the way, gay.

Uh-huh! You can't get away from it anywhere, not even on TV.

After the break they continued shooting with a new set-up. I was given my glass with its puddle of not-champagne and assumed my former position across from Bigmouth.

Barely a yard away, the moonfaced funeral director was standing with a lanky, good-looking guy, who talked to him and then hugged him.

I was standing in the middle of the shot; I could see the red light of the camera glowing between the two of them.

"I assume that's the boyfriend," I whispered to my companion.

"No, his brother."

The two let go of each other, and the red-haired guy shot us an irritated look.

"Is he gay, too?"

"Quiet please! And again: Rolling!" yelled the man in the chair, who couldn't possibly be the director because everybody knows that directors yell "Action!"

"Rolling!" someone echoed.

"No, he's got a girlfriend. But since the father's death, he's always hugging his brother and telling him he loves him. The guy's a little nuts."

I was on my feet for more than two hours, with an empty stomach and an empty glass, and moving my lips as intelligently as possible.

When I got home, I collapsed exhausted on my bed (once I had disposed of Paula's daily fax accompanied by Adam's letter). I promised myself that was my first and last day of shooting.

When it was aired half a year later, I noted with no small disappointment that the woman with the big mouth was on the screen three short times; me: only once; from behind.

"Are you by any chance missing your wallet?"

The redeeming phone call reached me as I was in the middle of working on my column. I was sitting at home because it was so hot outside that the slightest movement was too much.

The redeemer's name was Vince, and he had a slightly gravelly but overall nice voice, the type perhaps all wallet-finders have when you first speak with them.

He was sorry that he'd just gotten around to calling, but he hadn't been able to find my number until now (which was no big deal, since my new credit cards had come in the mail the day before).

I wanted to come over to his place to pick up my wallet, but he suggested that we meet in a French café on Melrose Avenue, where he was already sitting.

I knew the café. It was in among all those secondhand shops where they wanted forty-six dollars for a washed-out beige T-shirt; where Melrose Avenue seemed to be saying, "When I grow up, I'm going to be Carnaby Street. Or at the very least lead to Camden Town."

Vince waved to me as I came through the door. He was sitting between black-and-white photographs of the Eiffel Tower and the Champs-Élysées hanging on the wall.

"Good that you could come. You want something to drink?"

He looked familiar to me; I'd seen him a bunch of times at the Abbey.

Vince made a very studied impression: He was smooth-shaven, even his underarms. His large pores betrayed years of bad habits. Even his eyebrows were groomed and he smelled as if he had just bathed.

But it had been some time since his fingernails had seen a clipper; they were short, but chewed away into rough edges.

I ordered a coffee.

"So tell me something about yourself. Who are you?" Vince smiled at me.

"I don't mean to be impolite, but could I have my wallet back first?" I said.

"Absolutely! Sorry," he said, and reached into his jacket, which he had laid on the chair next to him. Then his telephone rang.

"Yeah ... Yeah, well that depends ... Sorry."

He needed to clear his throat, and politely put his hand in front of his mouth as he gave a brief cough.

Then he continued.

"Absolutely ... Today? Yeah, when? Where? One second."

He took a pen out of his jacket and neatly wrote an address in his datebook.

I looked out the window. A homeless guy, barely forty years old, stood by a garbage can, smoothing his shirt. He scoped out the entire area before he reached in.

"Excuse me, but I've gotta get going. Oh, this belongs to you."

Vince had ended his conversation, and handed me my wallet. He touched my hand briefly as he did, but wasn't looking at me.

I checked to see if anything was missing, but nothing was. It was nice to see Paula again.

"I don't want anything for it, but maybe we could go out for a drink sometime? You're gay, right?"

Again the cough. He took a quick swig from his cup.

I nodded and put the photo back in.

"Can I call you?"

I didn't say no, so I guess I said yes.

When he gave me a goodbye kiss on the cheek, I knew that something wasn't right. I checked the contents of my wallet for a third time, found the bare-torso picture of Adam from Joshua Tree National Park, but no explanatin. I paid for my coffee and went out on the street.

The homeless guy on the sidewalk threw a paper cup back into the garbage can, wiped his shirt with the flat of his hand a couple times, and moved long.

Adam and I had agreed to a half-hour break from talking in order to fully appreciate the peace of Joshua Tree National Park. Three hours away from Los Angeles by car, we were sitting on one of the hills and looking down into the valley.

Here the park consisted primarily of a bright brown steppe divided in two by a road that went through the vast area, upon which you occasionally saw a car. On either side grew isolated Joshua trees, which looked like cacti planted on top of defoliated trees.

When I opened my water bottle and held it at a slight angle, the wind blew past its neck and made a soft, hollow sound.

Otherwise it was so still that I was able to hear Adam's stomach growling. So he really was as hungry as he claimed when the no-talking period was over.

Just then a group of giggling local girls came tramping past, whom we had already seen at the visitors center and who greeted us perkily. It was like the Carpenters song:

That is why all the girls in town
Follow you all around

Just like me
They long to be
Close to you.

Adam was getting itchy, and finally we had to drive back to the hotel. First he thought that he had forgotten to lock the door of the apartment. When I assured him that I distinctly remembered turning the key twice, he tried other excuses.

"I don't think I turned the oven off properly. We should get back and check."

Or:

"Certainly they're going to close the park soon. I have no desire to spend the night here."

The actual reason for his panic was the sun, which was already determined to set and would soon be grazing the mountaintops. Adam would have done everything he could to avoid this view, including putting out his eyes or crawling into a burrow until it was all over.

"For all I care, you can close your eyes while the sun's setting, but I'm staying here until it's over."

My head was lying in his lap as the sun made its farewell peformance.

It lasted a nose-divey five minutes, during which it hurtled toward the horizon against a bright green sky, then submerged behind the mountains and finally disappeared, as if it had a secret pact with Adam to be done with it as quickly as possible today.

Then the real show began: The clouds had arrived. They bridged the time till the moon emerged, which had already been lurking in the background since the afternoon, like a diva awaiting her entrance, and later the stars.

Adam and I descended the mountain in silence.

In the sky, three long strips of cloud running parallel to the horizon overlapped one another and were gilded with the colors of the rainbow. Finally they settled into a softly glowing dark red in which they clearly felt most comfortable and were not to be driven from the stage.

But finally their time was up as well, and they drew back gray and unadorned into the background as the moon assumed its position.

We'd reached the road that led to our car. All around us it was dark night; the first stars were beginning to show.

Adam held a long, dried-out branch in his hand, with which he clopped the ground at regular intervals to scare off rattlesnakes that might be cozying up on the asphalt, storing up the day's heat.

"It's a bad time to get bit," the lady at the visitors center had warned us, and the girls behind us stopped giggling immediately.

"At the moment we're pretty short on antiserum. So if you come across a snake, keep talking to it and call the fire department; they'll trap it and take the poison out of it to make new antivenom."

My spontaneous counter-proposal that we go get a nonpoisonous coffee in nearby Palm Springs, the colony of the Polident People, the Baden-Baden Californians, was shot down by Adam. I shouldn't worry, he'd watch out for me.

I believed him, but inquired nonetheless why he'd never talked about this part of his life before, the part where he'd been on the road as a snake trainer with the Chinese state circus, which Adam didn't find particularly funny.

The night was mild and clear. Apparently they wanted to offer visitors to the park a few additional attractions: I had never seen so many stars in one cluster.

Unfortunately I couldn't really enjoy the view because I was keeping one eye nervously on the ground the entire way so as not to stumble upon a scorpion, a snake, or a sleeping coyote.

Unfortunately the road had been refinished with dark tar every few yards, so in the dark you never knew if that longish speck in the distance was a hungry wolf who had developed the bad habit of taking a late, light snack.

I had the impression that we were going in the wrong direction, but I didn't want to offend Adam in his role as tracker (and track finder). Besides, he seemed to be having a lot of fun telling me this story about the little boy whose parents forgot him during an outing in the park one day and who was never found again.

"And when you listen closely, you can hear him crying, very softly. Some people in the area even claim that they see him every year somewhere around the time his parents lost him. I think it must be around this time, today might even be the anniversary."

I didn't believe a word Adam was saying, but when suddenly a beam of light shot over the horizon, I jumped a little and grabbed onto Adam's arm, which he then pulled away, scaring me even more.

We had to laugh when the car drove slowly past us and the woman driving it looked at us as if we were two ghosts.

When we got to bed that night, Adam had another scare in store for me: He took my hand and said that he had seen worse sunsets than the one today, if I could imagine watching these kitschy shows nine hours after their broadcast in Germany, provided that he didn't always have to watch them with me.

I didn't have to wait long for Vince to call me. I'd barely been home two hours. Since I didn't have anything better planned, I got together with him for dinner (it also kept me from making an ill-advised visit to Adam; today was his birthday).

Vince had changed into a whole new set of clothes. He was wearing dark pants and a short white shirt. His cell phone was on the table in front of him. He stood up as I came into the restaurant, a few minutes late.

In the first ten minutes alone his phone rang three times. He got rid of the final caller by saying there was no way he could come over today. And no, not later, sorry.

"I'm sorry, it's always especially bad at night."

He was about to take my hand, which I had heedlessly laid on the table, but the waiter came to my rescue and took our order.

To minimize the space for Vince's sentimentality, I rattled on ceaselessly, told him about my stay in jail, my TV work, and about how much I liked Los Angeles.

Then he counted the number of times he'd seen me at the Abbey or at other bars. He even remembered which pants I wore where and when I hadn't shaved.

"One night you stood at the bar the whole time drinking martinis. Jordy, that's the name of the Spanish guy at the bar, the one with the long black hair, he bought you one later. It looked like you were waiting for someone, but later on you went home alone. You looked so sad."

At first I had to laugh at his stories, but then suddenly I felt threatened, as if he were holding a gun to my head. I wanted to put my hands up in the air and run away. For a while there I even thought that Adam had contracted him to keep an eye on me.

For sure: Vince was my secret observer; it was his eyes I could feel on me at the Abbey. I had found him out.

Just then his phone rang again, he wrote down a time and address on a coaster.

"So what do you do for money?" I asked him. I'd finally started to get suspicious.

He cleared his throat, perhaps a little longer than was necessary.

Then he said, "Different things. I work freelance. And you? Do you have brothers and sisters?"

He picked up his glass and brought it to his mouth without drinking from it. I regarded his shaved underarm with disgust.

"No. And that's the last question I'm answering tonight. What do you do for money? And who are these people who keep calling you?"

He set his glass down with a dull thud and looked at me as he nibbled at his index finger.

"Do you have to wreck everything?" he snapped at me. "Okay, I work with an escort service. Happy? I suck cock for money. Bad, I know. Now get up and run away like all the others."

I would have loved to ask him if he had worked as a pickpocket before retraining as a hustler, and whether his specialty had been wallets in men's pants pockets, but I had already stood up and was on my way out.

Finally the phantom was gone.

As I turned into Adam's street, I could see a light burning in his apartment. Certainly he had people over, a little birthday party. Brenda would be there, and the man with the gigantic teeth.

I wanted to turn around and go when Adam buzzed me in.

Why on earth had I rung the bell?

My stomach was churning like a washing machine in the spin cycle; I started to feel warm. I was trembling as I got into the elevator.

"I miss you, little guy," he had said in his letter, which Paula was still dutifully faxing me. Adam had written that over three months ago, but because I was reading it every day, it seemed very current.

All of sudden I could smell him. Probably he had just gotten home a little while ago. I closed my eyes and could feel myself getting warm and tight in my pants. Which annoyed me.

As I left the elevator I checked my reflection in the metal panel.

Adam looked at me like a little kid whose parents weren't home and who had just watched a film version of *The Wolf and the Seven Little Goats*, and chewed his lower lip nervously.

The precious black hair was shorter than before (I had noticed that already the time I saw him in Ultra Suede, when I pretended not to see him); he looked relaxed.

He let me in, but avoided any kind of contact: no look, no kiss, no touching. My heart was racing.

There was no one to be seen; apparently he was alone. The TV was playing in the background, an episode from one of those many comedy series I could never tell apart. One with a laugh track, so you knew when you were supposed to laugh. Someone was hiding behind a couch on which a couple was going at it, and apparently he was trying to get to a pink shirt that the woman and torn off the man and thrown on the floor.

On the wall were photos Adam had taken last winter when he was visiting me in Berlin. All the pictures lined up nicely next to each other, an orderly little row, the spaces between them measured with a ruler. In one photo I was wearing a scarf, a thick cap, and a hooded jacket; other than my nose, there was little of me to be seen. For some incomprehensible reason, Adam liked the picture. Why hadn't he taken it down long ago?

"How come you're here?"" he asked.

"It's a free country," I said, and felt how dry my throat was. It was difficult to swallow; you could hear it. Certainly Adam heard it, too.

Silence.

We stood there a few moments. He went to the window; looked out. I watched him. His left ear was trembling slightly.

Adam was a million miles away. I wanted to go to him, touch him.

Instead, I said softly:

"Why, Adam?"

Two small birds came up to the window, but then turned immediately away, as if they could sense the tension through the glass.

Adam leaned his forehead against the window; his breath was noticeably heavier, steaming the glass.

"Talk to me!"

The people on the TV bellowed.

Silence.

"I'm sorry."

More silence. Adam just kept looking down on the street.

"I'm sorry, Ben."

His voice became softer with every word; mine, louder: "Would you please turn around and tell me what happened?"

No reaction.

I jumped back when he suddenly burst out with: "I can't even explain it to you. I was so unbelievably excited about you coming; I wanted to cook something for us. In the afternoon I bought so much stuff that it almost didn't all fit in the refrigerator. My coworkers at the bank … they couldn't put up with my pining anymore. I was telling them all the time how many more days it was till you got here."

I wanted to say something, but Adam didn't let me.

"And when I was standing at the airport, all of a sudden I got into this panic. I was so terrified that we wouldn't have anything more to say to each other. That soon we'd start getting on each other's nerves in this apartment, and … that it was just a dumb, romantic idea."

Whinnying laughter from the TV.

"Is that all?"

"I thought maybe the only reason it was working out was because we saw each other so rarely. And don't they say it's better to end something while it's still at its peak?"

The audience applauded approvingly.

Nothing was going on in the room; it was as if the entire scene had frozen. As if someone, at the most suspenseful moment, had hit the pause button on the remote control.

I stood there like that for an hour, maybe a little less.

My throat was so dry that it hurt. Talking was impossible.

My leg began to shake.

Somewhere far, far away I saw Adam coming from the shower with a white towel wrapped around his hips. Beaming with joy, he lay down on the bed next to someone who looked like me.

I could hear the blood rushing through my head.

Suddenly something moved. Adam came up to me slowly, as if hurrying would be sacrilegious under the circumstances.

He stood in front of me for a moment; we looked at each other. His face drew nearer to mine, his lips were slightly open. I could hear him breathe. Or was that my own breath?

I lifted my hand slowly, and for a moment I stopped trembling. Then I cracked him a good one across the head and left the apartment.

Down on the street, I got really angry. I looked up at Adam's apartment. He was standing at the window.

I ran back and rang the bell.

Adam was holding a bag filled with ice cubes to his cheek as he opened the door.

"Happy Birthday," I said, and came in.

"Ben, I didn't want it to come to this. But ..."

"Okay, what really happened?"

"What?" He looked at me, clueless.

"What's his name? I saw him at the window."

"What's whose name?"

"Why did you even have me come in?"

"I'm sorry." Adam took the ice bag from his face and stared at it.

"If you say one more time that you're sorry, I'm gonna hit you again! Do you have any idea what I gave up for this! My job! I sold every fucking thing I had, I don't have anything anymore. Nothing. I have no life in Berlin at all anymore."

"I didn't know ahead of time."

"Then I'm just sitting around this city like some asshole, like some absolute idiot who's just too out of it to know what's going on. Then you sic this Brenda on me to do your dirty work for you."

Adam looked at me reproachfully.

"If you wouldn't always interrupt me ..."

"You do realize, don't you, that your story sounds totally insane."

"Nobody forced you to go to lunch with *Linda*," he said loudly, and put the ice packs back on his face. Then he took a deep breath. "Giving you the suitcase was her idea. She thought you'd need it. And so she picked it up before she met with you. I agreed to it because I wasn't capable of coming up with anything myself. Afterwards it was clear to me that you might take it funny. But then you couldn't be reached at the hotel. I went there once, but you had already left."

I felt like Adam was looking at me, but I couldn't return the look. I was boiling, I could've opened all the windows. The sudden silence was unbearable. Adam had turned off the TV.

"All of a sudden I just felt silly. And lonely. You were gone, and I couldn't talk to you anymore. Sure, I should have said something earlier; I knew that. But it just didn't happen. I thought I had to make up my mind all by myself. I missed you so much, little guy."

"Fuck you!" I yelled, and barged out of the apartment. Suddenly I was afraid. What was he talking about? I didn't understand a word.

In the hallway I nearly ran over Adam's neighbor, who apparently had been listening. She smiled at me innocently.

"The young man from Germany is back," she said.

The next night I got two surprising phone calls.

The first was from Gavin. We hadn't talked for a long time. Sure, I saw him at the theater every night, but somehow nothing ever came of it.

He'd get to the theater when I was already working, and I usually drove home as soon as I was done so I could listen to the answering machine.

"There's bad news. I don't know if you've heard yet."

He was calling me over a week after I'd tried to borrow a black suit from him, which now he didn't even mention.

First I found out that Gavin and his comedian boyfriend Ramon had broken up again (which I actually took as good news, but kept it to myself), before he came to the genuinely bad news.

The lease on the theater was going to be up in a few months, and there'd been a time when it could be renewed for ten more years. But the landlord, a little bald guy from Las Vegas who'd inherited the building from his parents, wasn't looking to renew. He wanted to sell the building at an outrageous price.

Which meant we needed a lot of money, but the banks weren't about to issue us a line of credit since no one harbored any great hope that a theater would ever turn a profit. No one seriously thought that people would suddenly develop a palpable need for American classics in which crazy dogs got shot, or for a modern version of *Arsenic and Old Lace* in which the old aunts have been turned into a lesbian couple. It was difficult enough to make these idiotic ideas sound original and witty in the press releases.

"Next week there's still one more meeting with a bank, but truth be told, it looks pretty much like we can all shoot ourselves at the farewell performance. At least that way we'll really fill the place."

It really was bad news, not least for my bank account. There wasn't much left of the money I'd earned selling my worldly goods (didn't I say fifty cents wasn't enough for a book!). The money I made at the theater slowed but didn't entirely stop my decline. Time for new job.

I thought about the funeral director with the red hair and wondered whether my future possibly lay in holding champagne glasses in poorly lit corners for sixty dollars a day, or maybe someday even being a black-and-blue, waterlogged corpse for eighty. Who knew what talents I possessed? Even Karen Carpenter had started out as the drummer in her brother's band, until they discovered she had this beautiful voice and a few years later she sang the number-one hit "Close to You."

"Wouldn't I make an uncannily good victim of the yellow fever?" I tried to joke, but it fell flat.

Gavin was very quiet while I told him about the TV shoot. And just as I wanted to ask him about my career possibilities as a horribly disfigured dead body, which an unsuspecting jogger comes across one morning on the edge of the woods; the act of a respectable bank employee who couldn't abide his ex-boyfriend's affair with a tall, attractive personal trainer, Gavin remembers he has an appointment. He has to go. Right in the middle of the most exciting part.

I had barely hung up when the phone rang again. Has to be Gavin, I thought, who's decided to listen to my grueling story to the end.

Instead: Silence.

"Gavin, is that you?" I asked. "Cut the shit. What's up?"

I got no answer.

"Hello?" I said again.

Nothing. Just breathing. Soft, regular breaths, so soft that I couldn't tell with any certainty whether they were a man's or a woman's.

For someone who wasn't used to punching people in the face, I really landed a beaut. Adam looked at me with his right eye; the left was dark red and swollen. He couldn't open it.

I felt sorry for him.

I'd driven over. I wanted to apologize. Although it was still difficult for me to believe his story. The guy with the big teeth still haunted my imagination. His being with another man seemed a much more plausible explanation.

It wasn't easy to picture Adam helpless. Certainly not panicky, not seeing a way out. I had never seen him like that.

Actually I didn't want to apologize. I drove over because he still had a couple of shirts and some CDs of mine.

He met me out in the hall, the apartment key in his hand. He'd closed the door behind him. Apparently it would open with as much difficulty as his swollen left eye.

"Am I not allowed in your apartment any more, Adam?"

He didn't move a muscle.

"What do you want?" he asked. His voice no longer had the softness that his confession had had two days before; he sounded hostile. He rattled the key in his hand anxiously.

"There's still some things inside that belong to me," I said amiably.

"I'd prefer to send them to you."

"I'd prefer to take them with me now."

Of course I hadn't come just for a couple of stupid shirts. I wanted to talk to Adam alone. In his apartment, not in front of it. Maybe in the kitchen with a glass of wine. Talk about old times: the weekend at Joshua Tree; the first time I met his parents. Maybe go into the living room and look at old photos. Look at each other. And then forget everything that's happened the past few months (I'd already begun by forgetting the affair with James; it works great).

But it seemed Adam was afraid I'd hit him again if he let me into the apartment.

"I'm not going away as easy as that," I said softly, and laid my hand on his shoulder. "And if you want to spend the night with me out here in the hallway—fine!"

It was a mistake.

While Adam got my shirts from the bedroom, I looked for a few CDs in the living room, which I found quickly since Adam had alphabetized them.

My every movement was observed by a thin guy with big teeth sitting on the couch with his legs crossed. He was eating an apple and pretending to read the newspaper. In the reflection from the TV screen I could see him craning his neck over the newspaper to gawk at me.

"Can I call you sometime?" Adam asked as he gave me my things in a plastic bag. I threw the CDs in, and went to the door. There, I extended my hand politely to Adam and said loudly:

"Tell your new boyfriend that next time he should hold the newspaper right side up."

CHAPTER 15

Nothing comes of trying to run away from your past, since:
—it follows you
—it's faster than you, and
—it might be your future

The Abbey was packed to the rafters; I'd much rather have turned around and left. I hated having to work my way through the masses of people; the appraising looks as you push past them. Sometimes I imagined that I was Moses and the parting crowd was my Red Sea, and behind me lurked an army of thousands of scantily clad Egyptian soldiers with freshly shaved chests—as a rule, this image was horrifying enough to bring me safely and quickly to my destination.

I was ten minutes late because I couldn't decide between the tight, white, short-sleeve shirt that showed off my nipples or the long-sleeve as well as boring shirt with the bright green stripes. Because I by no means wanted my reunion with James to prompt the idea, as I and my nipples would, of going to bed with him. On the other hand, Pete had once said about the green stripes, ohmygod, he could see borrowing the shirt if he wanted to give up eating eggs or if he had a job interview and was already sure there was no way he would take the job.

I decided on a simple sleeveless T-shirt, and just as the sea behind me swallowed up the brave Egyptians and I was breathing easier, I saw Adam. At first just from behind, but that was enough, since I'd so often woken up and had my glance fall first to the back of that head with its full, thick, black hair and onto his small ears.

I was also sure that even if he had been standing behind a wall, I would have sensed his presence—yeah, practically smelled it.

But what in god's name was he looking for here? Had he come to torpedo my reunion with James? On the other hand, maybe he didn't know a thing about it.

A group of two or three men was standing around him; one of them was relating an adventure from the previous weekend so loudly that even with the music you could still hear him two blocks away. The others listened patiently

Adam wasn't the type to be always checking out the immediate vicinity when he was out somewhere with someone. Nothing and no one distracted him, and he didn't stare at the ass of every guy who pushed past him to the bathroom. So I could have easily slipped off (though the Moses routine often can't be repeated) without Adam having ever known.

But that wouldn't work. Should I move forward or backward, and which direction was backward anyway? To go or to stay? I looked hectically around me, like a squirrel in Surprise Valley surrounded by a dozen hunters who wouldn't be happy until they'd taken out at least a hundred.

Where was I? And far more important: Why?

The center of the solar system?

Earth, of course. Stupid question.

The audience watched me, stunned. Some turned their backs on me; others began to laugh. Was that Vince I saw in the back, biting his nails? I reached into my pants pocket and grabbed my wallet.

"Hey, where're you from?" someone called to me and laid his hand on my shoulder. "You're totally pale. Just landed, huh?"

It was like the pistol shot for a hurdler. I ran off, just wanted to get out, be alone, pack my bag, die, run off, enter a convent.

There was a horrible rumble and crash when I ran into the waiter, who was just about to serve some food. The people at the table jumped up in horror, a bottle fell and rolled off the table to shatter on the tile floor. Three hungry pairs of eyes regarded me with disgust. A huge commotion with much yelling and shouting. And all around us music, an old Eurythmics song which I would have loved to hear under other circumstances. All conversation had been silenced.

I looked for a moment at the mishmash of broken plates, leaves of lettuce and fried potatoes, mumbled something that sounded like "I'm sorry!" and quickly stuck a couple broken pieces back together. Then ran for the exit, where I bumped into the doorman. He grabbed my arm and wanted to hold onto me, but I pulled myself free of him and ran into the street. Cars honked as I suddenly popped up in front of them; one driver got out and called something after me that I couldn't make out. A red jeep with squealing tires came to a standstill right at my feet; the woman driving it leaned out her window and gave me the finger.

I turned a corner and rammed into a couple holding hands as they stood in front of the display window of a furniture store. The impact made me lose my balance and I fell to the ground. Scathing looks from the woman. The man shook his head and pulled her closer to him.

As I jumped up, I felt a painful stab in my wrist, but continued running. Someone was behind me. Or was I just hearing the echo of my own steps? But can an echo suddenly speed up?

I tried to run faster, even though my foot hurt.

"Stop already!" a familiar voice yelled. "Please!"

It gave me such a start that I automatically slowed down.

Then I felt a hand on my shoulder, and stopped.

"Ben, what the fuck are you doing?"

Adam brought me to his car. There he cleaned out the cut on my hand and stuck a band-aid on it.

I watched him as he was doing it. His left eye was yellowish green, and he could open it again. When he looked up at me, I quickly turned away.

"Does that hurt?" he asked, and pulled my fingers; he tried bending them back and forth.

I pulled my hand away from him and looked at him angrily.

"Yes, that hurts, too, thank you very much. It seems to amuse you."

"You should get that to a doctor tomorrow. I can drive you if you like."

"Thanks, but I can manage," I said.

"I don't know if that's advisable with a sprained wrist."

"If you already know that it's sprained, then I don't need to go to the doctor."

He stowed the first aid kit behind his seat and extended his hand to me.

"I'll drive you home. Or to the hotel. Where exactly are you staying?"

"Not necessary. My car's right near here."

With that I turned and made to go.

He shut the door and leaned on the car.

"Were you here the entire time?"

I turned my back on him again and nodded.

"You're crazy."

My throat was as dry as the San Diego freeway after two months without rain. The words were stuck in my throat like the traffic on the freeway when it finally rains after two months and the Los Angelinos are utterly overwhelmed.

I jump into Adam's arms and revel in the way he strokes my hair and passionately kisses me.

But that was just a momentary thought.

Happy endings only exist in Hollywood. Paula was right.

"Do you have a job?" he asked.

I turned to him.

"The newspaper."

We stood looking at the ground in front of us for a long time. The street was paved with that weirdly interesting black-gray Los Angeles asphalt.

"Why did you come over to see me that night? Certainly not just because of a couple of CDs."

I briefly considered finally apologizing for the black eye. Instead I asked:

"Why were you sitting home all alone on your birthday?"

"Are you … have you met anyone?" he asked in turn, in order to avoid answering my question.

A car pulled up slowly; the window went down. Two guys wanted to know how to get to Revolver, a bar in the neighborhood that was showing *Queer as Folk* on the big screen.

Grateful, I told them how to get there.

The driver alternately stared at the spots of blood on my shirt and at my pants, the side of which had gotten torn when I took my tumble. Then he saw Adam's black eye and grinned, but he didn't drive on.

"Anything else?" I snapped at them.

Finally they left.

"Where are you living?" Adam asked.

I told him about Robert and the dog that was so ugly that he'd been castrated when he was just a few months old to reduce his aggressive tendencies (the official reason) and to prevent the propagation of his breed (my theory).

"It's a shame you didn't return my calls," he said softly, and stuck his hands deep in his pockets the way he did that time on Venice Beach before he asked me to have something to eat with him.

At that moment I wished Adam would start moving around the fingers on my sprained wrist again. That was a pain I could deal with.

"I also wrote to you," he said.

"Yeah."

"The guy in my apartment—that wasn't anybody. Just a friend."

"It would really mean a lot to Adam if the two of you could be friends," I could hear Brenda saying.

"Uh-huh."

"I'm sorry that I wrecked everything," Adam said softly.

"We've already been there, Adam."

He slammed his fist against the door, and took a step toward me.

"Goddamit, could we maybe just talk to each other normally?"

"Why? To make you feel better about everything? So go talk to Brenda or to—"

"Her name is Linda. You never did like her," Adam said.

"Or the guy with the teeth. That is, if you've managed to put up with him longer than ten days at a stretch. In that case: Congratulations!"

"You're suffering from a persecution complex, Ben."

"And if nothing's going on with him anymore," I screamed on, undeterred, "then you can simply send Brenda out again."

Adam stood stock still in front of me, and it looked like the moment when he might avenge his black eye. But he jumped into his car and started the engine.

We looked at each other silently for a while through the pane of glass. Adam's face glowed dark red; the veins beneath his eyes were sticking out. Finally he turned off the engine. He leaned back and closed his eyes.

I could have run off. Better put: hobbled off, since my foot still really hurt—which I didn't feel that until later.

Adam wouldn't have noticed that I simply wasn't there any longer. I could have driven home in peace, had a nice evening, maybe even been talked into taking an unattractive dog for a walk around the block (as I said, at the moment my foot still felt quite normal), the leash in the left hand, the obligatory plastic bag in the right for picking up his turd. Or I could have had a nice dinner with Robert; maybe he'd found me some more jobs as an extra where I could be hit on by red-haired funeral directors; maybe I'd kill him after supper with the feeding dish of the world's ugliest dog because he made a snide remark about Adam. I also could have gone back to the Abbey, apologized for the minor accident; maybe still even run into James there. Otherwise there was always the possibility of meeting a nice young man who'd stick his tongue in my ear (the smaller of the two) as he whispered that I looked to be twenty-one at the most, to which I'd reply that he should see me in daylight; and when he woke up next to me the morning after, he'd agree with me and run to the bathroom for half an hour. Or I could have, given the circumstances, gone to the airport and gotten a cheapo last-minute return ticket for the next day (or would that wreak havoc with the luggage cabal: Could they get their people moving so quickly?)

So, Adam thought I was suffering from a persecution complex? That was more than ridiculous.

He couldn't have a normal conversation with me? Absurd!

Like always. Suddenly I found myself in his car again, breathing heavily, half next to him, half on top of him, maybe even a bit under him.

Language lacks just one clear preposition to exactly describe co-ital positions initiated from the passenger seat. A pity: Noah Webster came out with his *Compendious Dictionary of the English Language* in 1806; the first gasoline-powered car didn't appear in the U.S. until 1893. If Noah could have waited just 87 years, he and Mrs.

Webster could have gone for a test drive, and today prepositions like "underbove" and nextonto" wouldn't seem so strange.

We didn't talk anymore; we didn't even try. Finally it had happened. We had both wanted it, and now it was embarrassing for us.

In order to defog the glass, we drove back to my car with the windows down. I felt like I was fourteen. As we drove, I thought about how I was going to explain to my parents why I was getting home so late.

"Baby, we were so worried. But what's happened to your hand?"

Adam stopped next to my car. He kept the motor running and looked at me.

Had I inadvertently said earlier that Earth was the center of the solar system? Of course that was total nonsense. It was right here, next to me, in this car.

Okay! Lock it in!

"So then, good night," he said, as the choir took its breath for a second round of "Close to You."

"You still have to ask for my telephone number."

I was so angry at myself for that that I could have thrown myself in front of the next passing car.

"I don't know," he said, and looked at the street.

I found a pen in the glove compartment and a map of the city, on which I wrote my number.

Then I thanked him for his help and bid him a good night.

"Maybe that was a mistake," he said, and continued looking out over the steering wheel.

I could have screamed in pain when I set my foot on the street.

July was coming to an end; it had gotten so warm in Los Angeles that you preferred to stay in your cool apartment during the day. The air outside was dry and hot and filled with the hum of air conditioners running at full speed. During the summer, the watering of public lawns guzzled the annual water requirements of entire African countries.

Those who could, drove to the beach where, on the other hand, it could be so cool that you needed a jacket, even though you had barely driven ten miles.

I lay on the bed trying without success to fold the *National Enquirer*, and finally just laid it on my lap. Sighing, I closed my eyes.

With my left hand I reach for the chocolate on the nightstand. It's sitting between the strawberries and the pitcher of freshly squeezed orange juice.

Adam has seen to everything.

"Leave the newspaper, little guy. I'll do that in a second," he calls over from the desk.

Sighing again, I let myself drop back, and look at the plaster cast on my arm. Everyone has already been to visit and signed it: Pete, Scott, Gavin, Brenda, even James. "A shame!" he wrote in parentheses after his name.

"Is 'Aniston' spelled with one 'n' or two," the sweet man asks and turns to me.

"And what does the article say, how much did the house cost? 12 or 21 million?"

He's typing my column for me until the cast is finally taken off. He's taken a couple extra days off.

Adam had spoken on the phone with Carstensen earlier and gotten rid of him. He had only wanted to let me know how much he liked my last few pieces, he wrote me later in an e-mail.

And how happy he was to infer from his conversation with the American gentleman that I had taken his advice (this referred to one of his earlier tantrums in which he had recommended in a friendly way that I get thoroughly fucked so that I might start writing clever pieces again).

"I think it was twelve. *Hmm, twelve. Oh well..* But I'll read it though again."

Adam comes over to me and sits down next to me.

"Do you need anything?"

He kisses my brow, and strokes my cheek tenderly.

I hum contentedly to myself.

Why do birds suddenly appear
Every time you are near?

I opened my eyes and saw my empty room.

No Adam to be seen; no Adam to be heard. I'd waited days for his call. It was all starting over again.

I considered it impossible that he was behind some calls I'd received recently. Usually at night. Whoever it was never said anything, at least not with words. It was always just this breathing. And then it would get faster. It developed into panting and moaning. The caller scared me. Did he know what I looked like? Did he know my address?

It wasn't Adam, that much was certain (he never moaned before he came).

I thought I heard familiar voices: "I'm sorry I messed everything up."

"It would really mean a lot to Adam if the two of you could be friends."

"Happy endings only exist in Hollywood."

The *National Enquirer* was lying on my lap; next to me was a bunch of other newspapers and a bottle of water. On the computer's screen saver a few brightly colored fish were swimming here and there.

My glance fell on the suitcase next to the desk. Then I threw the newspaper under my bed and reached for the phone.

The woman at the travel agency asked me cheerfully what she could do for me.

CHAPTER 16

Living with a woman promises to be good and pleasant:

—even if she can't make coffee

—even if no hair will grow on her chest

—even if she's thrown out your valuable collection of Lorenzo Lamas posters instead of hanging onto them as promised

So Matlock went. A small Mexican family got him, even if they couldn't or wouldn't pay the price I was asking. Strictly speaking, they talked me down to about half (I was unpleasantly reminded of my Berlin flea market experience), but I preferred that to giving my car to a pierced-tongue teenager I had sent away the day before.

The little daughter with sparkling black eyes waved to me from the rear window as they drove off in my car (when I was cleaning it out, I finally found my map of the city under the passenger seat).

"And now we go shopping!" Scott exclaimed and massaged my shoulder. Then he kissed me on the mouth, as usual, with his lips slightly open.

I smiled at him. If he thought I was one of those sentimental people who mourned the loss or sale of a canopied couch on wheels, he was wrong.

We were shopping for a small party on Sunday. A few people wanted to come to the theater after the performance for drinks: Scott and Pete, maybe James, and of course all the actors and tech people were also invited. And when I flew back to Germany early the next week, Mrs. Spring would take over my job until they found someone to write the program notes and sell the final tickets through the end of the year.

Paula had already set up some appointments to look at apartments.

"So you don't get the idea again of letting someone come on to you at the last minute. You know, you're needed here. Daniel is really looking forward to seeing you. Did you call him yet?"

"I haven't been able to get around to it yet," I answered.

That wasn't entirely untrue. There was a massive amount of things to get in order.

For example, I had spoken with Carstensen. The woman he had hired after I left was pregnant and would soon be taking maternity leave.

"I'm telling you, she had barely signed the contract when she gets knocked up on the very next street corner!"

He had a clear idea about who should take over her job.

"Not like you'll be getting any ideas about procreating, too, now. First you have to look for a man who can put up with you."

I hadn't really planned on either of these, but even less did I want to get back into the editorial grind with its bully-session meetings, its office gossip, its waiting for return phone calls from press reps, who in the end do nothing but repeat what was said in the press release anyway.

I'd sat out in the park too often with my computer, next to me a large cup of my favorite latte, the sun above me; in front of me a pair of pushy squirrels gawking at me with big, black eyes; behind me a Japanese woman who was training her dog by chasing it back and forth across the grass until it nearly collapsed after ten minutes and had to be carried back to the car.

Nobody was going to have an easy time of it getting me back into an office, where the phone was always ringing; where utterly witty colleagues put up funny signs like: "Employees who come in later in the day are asked to keep to the right so as not to collide with colleagues who leave earlier in the afternoon."

Or:

"Oh, it's good our boss is there—and not here."

Apart from that, Carstensen's attacks of choler were infinitely easier to bear on the phone than at a morning staff meeting where you sat with an empty stomach because yet again you hadn't had time for breakfast.

I refused his offer, but promised to have lunch with him as soon as I was back in Germany.

And everything was okay with Gavin again.

As it turned out, his problem wasn't envy. Rather, on the day my extra-star rose and set with the sun, he had to go to the funeral of an ex-boyfriend. And, thinking that he had told me about it, when I called to borrow his black suit for the same day in order to hold my champagne glass with more dignity, he'd have loved to bury me as well.

I invited him to my house for dinner. We had pizza.

Just a little while ago I had discovered this place that delivers where they had enormous pizzas that, unlike their competitors, didn't consist of 99% dough. They were topped with the best sausage and the finest olives—and the delivery guys weren't exactly unappetizing themselves.

The pizza I made that night all by myself was considerably less tasty, but two years with Adam had taught me my way around a kitchen, and Gavin raved at length about the delicate shapes into which I had cut the mushroom slices.

We hadn't finished eating yet when I heard Robert's key in the door.

He was coming from one of his house calls, and looked exhausted but satisfied. The three of us knocked off a couple bottles of wine.

Gavin talked about the Woody Allen concert he'd been to a couple of nights before: a surprise appearance at a small club. One of the waitresses, by whom he was also served at home on a regular basis, had told him about it.

"The guy usually doesn't even come to Los Angeles to accept his Oscars, and here he was that night, playing his clarinet for an hour. It was crazy."

Something about Woody Allen playing clarinet reminded Robert of the previous hours of his evening, which he shared with us in elaborate detail.

When I figured I'd had enough of hearing about the motor skills of his date's tongue and wanted to change the subject, I started talking to Gavin about what was happening with the theater, and found out that the deadline had been pushed back a week.

It may well have been our blood alcohol level or Robert's post-orgasmic hormonal boost, but that evening we came up with an insane idea:

We wanted to rent out the theater two or more days a week, ideally Friday and Saturday, to a party organizer who Robert knew personally. So a business plan that would convince the banks had to be developed as quickly as possible. Robert also saw these evenings as a way to look out for new faces for the agency; for a few dollars they could record their own personal application in a kind of video machine (and who knows, maybe this way he'd find a natural talent who could wind her tongue all the way around the neck of a champagne bottle).

As I was packing my bags my last weekend there, my thoughts wandered to the fat little guy and his scraggly cohort with the overbite. Were they still in the city? Maybe they'd send colleagues of theirs to annoy me this time instead. After all, it was the middle of August, vacation time, and maybe one of them had children and wasn't available despite a commitment of many years to his victim. But this year—Sorry! Someone should have let him know earlier.

I was kind of anxious about going back, but not because of those guys.

Where were the friends who had stopped e-mailing me after just a few weeks, stopped calling entirely? Would they suddenly resurface, and had they changed? Was I the same?

What'll I do with my blahs when there's no real sunlight for days on end and it rains five weeks in a row? Maybe I'll start creeping along the autobahn like a Los Angelino, terrified of wet pavement.

A life without an extra portion of sunshine every day.

Can I get used to the bad moods of German waiters again? Granted, "Hi, my name is Arne, and I will be your waiter" sounds odd, but couldn't they at least try?

Who will pack my bags when I go grocery shopping, and keep me from killing the cashier when instead of greeting me with a cheery "Hi, how are you? Did you find everything you were looking for?", she grunts "This lane is closed!"

Well, I had Paula. She was all I needed for a new beginning. And her couch. We had each other. And we had our best friend Martina.

It'd all work out.

The telephone tore me away from my thoughts. It was an old acquaintance.

"Hhhhhhhheeeeewwwww…"

The palms of my hands began to sweat; the phone nearly slipped from my hand. The moaning grew louder; I wanted to hang up. The disturbance had made my breathing get faster, and I was afraid he'd take it as a sign of arousal. I held my breath.

Suddenly it was quiet, just for a moment. A short cough, as if he'd choked on something; then he cleared his throat, and the game continued. Gradually his breathing sped up again.

But I had recognized him.

"I should have known," I said after a while, and could feel how I was slowly getting calmer and more collected.

The moaning didn't stop. It would still be a little while till orgasm. I had been forced to become familiar with his habits.

I could see him in front of me, the regular movement of clean-shaven underarm getting faster and faster. It was disgusting.

"Do you really take money for that?" I asked.

He didn't react; maybe he couldn't understand me anymore. His moaning had become loud and vocal—and easily recognized. Why had it taken me so long?

"I'm flying back to Germany in a few days," I said. "What're you going to do without me, Vince?"

Vince hung up.

I was looking forward to my going away party, and it was a lovely evening. All the important people had come, and of course the people from the theater.

The funny thing about actors was that they often continued playing their roles when they were offstage. That is, they'd incorporate quotes from their current play into every little conversation, adapting them as necessary and having great fun with it.

The annoying thing about actors was that this sort of thing gets on your nerves very quickly when you've seen the shows at least three times.

A small sample:

Pete was holding an empty glass in the air and asking where the wine bottles were stowed.

The director answered:

"Oh sweetie, look in the window seat."

That was originally from an exchange between the aunts/lesbians in *Arsenic and Old Lace*, referring to the resting place of one of their latest victims, as I explained to Pete. Among the actors it had the status of a tag line, and brought the director peals of laughter and appreciative slaps on the back.

Pete looked at me, clueless, but laughed along out of courtesy.

Scott uncorked a new bottle, and said not to worry, there were still at least twelve left, red and white both.

"Hmm, twelve? Well …," screamed two of the actors in unison and then doubled over in laughter.

When someone asked about Gavin ("Hmmtwelvewell" was his line), who said he was coming but hadn't appeared yet, Mrs. Spring, my Texan successor, said someone should give him a call, maybe he'd just fallen asleep at home.

"Call? He's right over the river. It'd be quicker if I'd swim!"

Two more points for the director.

Pete, bored, stared at the ceiling and ran his hand for the second time through his thinning hair.

I spared telling him any more quotes, and turned to Robert. He was trying, apparently without success, to convince Roshumba (the overall-wearing lesbian from *Arsenic and Old Lace*) to come see him at the agency.

He greeted me with a grin that I couldn't quite read. Roshumba rolled her eyes as she disappeared behind Robert and was given some wine by Scott.

"You seem to be particularly happy that soon you'll never see me again," I said.

"Don't talk bullshit! I did a good deed today, that's all."

Robert grinned widely.

"Did you finally find work for a woman who hadn't slept with you?"

"Okay, Ben, so when exactly is your flight?"

Robert didn't mean it seriously. And he took nobody seriously, except himself. This made living with him very difficult at times. Nonetheless, I'd miss him and his hideous dog.

My stomach felt like just one solid, heavy lump, gasping for air. I took a deep breath, sighed, and took a big gulp of wine.

"Another victim of the yellow fever!" someone yelled as my comedian-lawyer, Ramon, lost his balance dancing and found himself with some surprise in the strong arms of one of the lighting guys, whom he thanked with a long kiss.

He'd given me a pair of handcuffs covered in lime green plush as a going away present.

The card that came with them said: "What are you going to do without me when you're in Germany and you get into trouble again?"

Pete forced me to dance with him when someone put a Madonna CD on, and sang: "It doesn't matter if you're black or white, if you're a boy or a girl."

Then he threw his arms around my neck.

"Honey, won't you just think it over one more time? What's Berlin got that L.A. hasn't?"

"Naked dance parties. Forgotten already?" I said, and truly regretted that soon no one would call me "honey."

"You can come back any time, your room will always be available. Although …" He seemed to be thinking about something. "It could be that Scott may have to move there first if he keeps nibbling on the ear of that Sean Penn wannabe. 'Little miss thinks she can have whatever she wants in the blink of an eye.'"

Scott had been talking very intensely for a while with the conceited actor who played crazy Teddy in the play and had to bury the two lesbians' victims in the basement.

I thought of Scott's body in the basement, Jacksonorjason, who stroked his hair behind his ear as he sucked at the straw in his salt-less margarita. Maybe I shouldn't have left the two of them alone that night.

"They're just talking," I said.

"He had also 'just talked' with that other little twink before he got into his pants. Y'know?"

With a panicky movement of his hand, Pete wiped the thin, black hair out of his face (it had taken on a slightly reddish tone that you could see when you stood really close to him), and pulled me to the bar.

There he filled two glasses to the rim with wine. He drank half his glass in one gulp, and poured himself some more right after.

A group of actors whistled and applauded as the door opened and a large bouquet of flowers entered, behind which Gavin was concealed.

The music was suddenly turned off; someone yelled, "Everybody gather round: half-circle!" and the lighting guy temporarily took his hand out of Ramon's pants.

Gavin handed Roshumba the flowers and looked at the circle of people.

"So you little shits, I know it's difficult for you, but maybe you could shut up for about five minutes."

A couple actors whistled; someone yelled that they should put the music back on, but please not the Madonna CD again.

Gavin scratched his temple with his little finger and cleared his throat.

"Apparently that was a pretty shitty intro. Okay, Take Two: As some of you know, I've just come from meetings about our little home here, and the way it looks … it looks really good. I can't give much more away right now, just this: The banks love our idea; we didn't give them any choice."

A few actors applauded; a woman whistled through her fingers.

"Well, the idea wasn't just my baby, even if I'd like to say so."

Gavin's glance roamed the crowd until it finally settled on me. I'd have gladly shared his optimism, but maybe I wasn't drunk enough, or mentally was halfway back to Berlin already.

With a short wave of his hand he beckoned me to come to him.

"Unfortunately one of the three fathers of the baby has decided to pick up and take off and leave all the work to us. So now I'm gonna call for a vote: Everybody who thinks that there's just no way Ben can go, raise your hand."

I think the vote was unanimous, but my vision had gotten blurry and I hid my face first behind the bouquet of flowers, and then in Gavin's arms.

"Now you have to say you accept the vote," he whispered to me.

Scott handed me my glass, which I gratefully accepted. I took a gulp, and looked at all the faces around me. They didn't make it easy for me.

"You're very sweet. And I hope I can still keep the bouquet if I stick to my decision?"

Gavin punched me in the side and grinned.

"And could somebody please hurry up and put the music back on?" I yelled.

Mrs. Spring brought a bucket of water for the flowers, and pressed me to her breast. She wished me much happiness and said good-bye.

Someone was taking care of the music, the party was warming up again. Suddenly Scott was standing behind me and laid his arms around my neck.

I held his hand for a moment, and felt the tears wanting to come back.

"You want Pete to kill me out of jealousy in my last moments here?" I asked, my back to him.

"I'll be the first one he'll kill anyway. Did you see the looks he was giving me when I was talking with that actor? Who has very pretty eyes, by the way, but I'm not his type."

I could feel his mustache as he was whispering in my ear. It tickled, but wasn't unpleasant.

"Yeah, unfortunately I was never your type."

Before I could say anything in response, I heard Pete's clamoring voice, and Scott let go of me. I didn't see where they went because I was pulled by both arms onto the dance floor.

I was sandwiched right between Gavin and an actor when Mrs. Spring reappeared.

"There's someone at the door for you."

"Why doesn't he come in?"

"He said he'd rather talk outside."

Robert clapped me on the shoulder as I ran past him to the exit and yelled something after me that I couldn't understand.

I got out on the sidewalk and looked around. Nobody was there. Mrs. Spring must have been mistaken.

All the parking spaces in front of the theater were taken. Pleasure seekers crept along Sunset Boulevard in their cars. Far off, police sirens could be heard.

I looked into the sky. Just then a shooting star fell, or maybe it was just a helicopter making a turn. A thick cloud moved along, giving a view of the full moon.

Paula was sure to be just sitting down to breakfast, drinking her weak coffee and reading the newspaper. She had probably already prepared her couch—my couch—and put two bottles of vermouth, white and red, on ice. We'd knock them off with our martinis later in the evening, after our welcome-home champagne for twelve marks (hmm, twelve; well …) up in the television tower, with the best view of Berlin.

A cool wind blew between the buildings and through the mesh of my shirt, and gave me goosebumps.

Had I understood Scott correctly earlier, that he wasn't my type? Was that a belated come-on? And why now? Or had I been blind the entire time? His open-mouthed kisses …

I was about to go back in when a familiar song sounded from across the street. Whenever a car drove by, it would be drowned out.

Why do birds …
… you are near
Just like me they want …

I closed my eyes, leaned against the wall of the building, and breathed in the music and the cold night air.

… stars fall down from …
… walk by

The volume increased just for a moment as a car door was opened and then closed again.

"Maybe I can get used to this song eventually, little guy," Adam yelled, and suddenly popped up next to his pickup.

He was wearing a bright polo shirt with just one button open, but even at a distance I could still make out clearly the dark thick hair on his chest.

Adam starts crossing the street, then stops halfway and looks at me.

Approaching from the left is one of those black stretch limos in which one always imagines stars like Russell Crowe or Jennifer Lopez with her hot ass, but which usually are just carrying tourists being chauffeured around the city. It's easy to not see these black monstrosities at night, even though this stretch of Sunset Boulevard is well-lit.

Some cars parking in front of me block my view; I'm just as surprised as Adam and can't warn him.

I first notice the limousine when the driver hits its brakes and it comes to a stop with screeching tires a few yards later.

I close my eyes, but I still see blood. There's a horrible amount of blood, and it mixes in with the skid marks, is virtually burned into the pavement by the tires. When the limousine finally comes to a halt, I think I hear Adam's relieved sigh, happy that this last, unwanted journey has finally come to an end.

Almost at the same time something lands on the ground next to me with the dull squoosh of a wet towel. It's an arm; in the dark I can't make out whether it's his left or his right. Strictly speaking, it doesn't really make a difference.

I see people fall to their knees on the sidewalk, crying; others raise their arms pleading to heaven, stunned and reproachful that this innocent young man of all people had to be singled out for this.

A wary smile appears on my face.

The light from the streetlamps hurts my eyes at first when I open them. Slowly the noise of the traffic swells again; all of Los Angeles seems to be on the move tonight.

A cool wind is still blowing between the buildings, but I'm not freezing anymore. I sense a pleasant warmth all through my body; I feel Adam's hand on my shoulder and, relieved, I hear his voice:

"I hope I didn't come too late."

CREDITS

Page 48: "The show is over, say good-bye."
from: "Take a Bow"; *Bedtime Stories* (Madonna)

Page 111: "Pain is a warning that something's wrong."
from: "The Power of Good-bye"; *Ray of Light* (Madonna)

Page 118: "Once you put your hand in the flame/You can never be the same."
from: "Erotica"; *Erotica* (Madonna)

Page 118: "Ooops, I didn't know we couldn't talk about sex."
from: "Human Nature"; *Bedtime Stories* (Madonna)

Page 122: "If you have to ask for something more than once or twice, it wasn't yours in the first place."
from: "Waiting"; *Erotica* (Madonna)

Page 198: "It doesn't matter if you're black or white, if you're a boy or a girl"
from: "Vogue"; *I'm Breathless* (Madonna)

Page 198: "Little miss thinks she can have what she wants in a blink of an eye."
from: "Thief of Hearts"; *Erotica* (Madonna)

various quotes from:
"Close to You"; *Interpretations: A 25th Anniversary Celebration* (The Carpenters)

… and my thanks go to:

—**Maria Roxane** for reading this and re-rereading this and reading it one more time
—**Peter Rehberg** for the jubilant text message after the first 40 pages
—**Rainer Marek** for liking it
—**Yasmine Ghandtchi**
—**Anke Wilmesmeyer**
—**Caroline Sendele**
—**Tarek Ibrahim** for cruising me on Santa Monica Boulevard
—**Kai Karsten + Dorsy Baumgartner**

—**Burt Bacharach** (music) and **Hal David** (lyrics) for "Close to You"